PRAISE FOR SUSAN HATLER

"I couldn't help but smile and laugh at the antics that Ben and Sarah go through. I'm so excited for this whole series!"
— *Katie's Clean Book Collection re The Wedding Charm*

"Ms. Hatler has a way of writing witty dialogue that makes you laugh-out-loud throughout her stories."
— *Night Owl Reviews*

"I am a huge fan of Susan Hatler!!! I have yet to read a book I did not absolutely love!"
— *Tifferz Book Reviewz*

"Hatler is my go-to girl for a sizzling clean romance with swoon-worthy kisses!"
— *Books Are Sanity!!!*

"Susan Hatler *writes books that sit right in my sweet spot and make me happy.*"
— *Getting Your Read On Reviews*

"An Unexpected Date is a wonderful and perfect release to a stressful or crazy day."
— *Cafè of Dreams Book Reviews*

TITLES BY SUSAN HATLER

Do-Over Date Series
Million Dollar Date
The Double Date Disaster
The Date Next Door
Date to the Rescue
Fashionably Date
Once Upon a Date
Destination Date
One Fine Date
The Date Mistake

The Wedding Whisperer Series
The Wedding Charm
The Wedding Catch
My Wedding Date
The Wedding Bet
The Wedding Promise

Blue Moon Bay Series
The Second Chance Inn
The Sisterhood Promise
The Wishing Star
The Friendly Cottage
The Christmas Cabin
The Oopsie Island
The Wedding Boutique
The Holiday Shoppe

Better Date than Never Series
Love at First Date
Truth or Date
My Last Blind Date
Save the Date
A Twist of Date
License to Date
Driven to Date
Up to Date
Déjà Date
Date and Dash

Christmas Mountain Romance Series
The Christmas Compromise
'Twas the Kiss Before Christmas
A Sugar Plum Christmas
Fake Husband for Christmas

Treasured Dreams Series
An Unexpected Date
An Unexpected Kiss
An Unexpected Love
An Unexpected Proposal
An Unexpected Wedding
An Unexpected Joy
An Unexpected Baby

Young Adult Novels
See Me
The Crush Dilemma
Shaken

THE CHRISTMAS COMPROMISE

SUSAN HATLER

The Christmas Compromise
Copyright © 2018 by Susan Hatler

All rights reserved. Without limiting the rights under copyright reserved above, no part of this publication may be reproduced, stored in or introduced into a retrieval system, or transmitted, in any form, or by any means (electronic, mechanical, photocopying, recording, or otherwise) without the prior written permission of the copyright owner of this book. This is a work of fiction. Names, characters, places, brands, media, and incidents are either the product of the author's imagination or are used fictitiously.

ISBN: 9781792075094

Cover Design by Elaina Lee, For The Muse Design
www.forthemusedesign.com

** To receive a FREE BOOK , sign up for
Susan's Newsletter:
susanhatler.com/newsletter **

THE CHRISTMAS COMPROMISE

SUSAN HATLER

CHAPTER ONE

As I drove down the highway toward my hometown of Christmas Mountain, my heart fluttered with anticipation—a second later, however, an ice-cold feeling of anxiety rushed through my veins. I was coming home to Montana on my *own* terms to live my *own* life, but as soon as my mom found out about my change in career paths a war would ensue.

My mouth went dry thinking about the impending conversation with my mom. I'd tell her the truth. She'd be disappointed in me. I'd feel bad. Then I'd revert back to pleasing her....

Except, *no*. Not this time.

I gripped the steering wheel hard. I was twenty-six years old and entitled to make my own decisions. Besides, it's not like I could keep my new beauty salon a secret in our small town even if I wanted to. While I'd lived in Florida, I'd kept my secret running on two years now—the ginormous fact that I'd passed on the MBA program and used my inheritance money to attend the beauty academy instead.

I couldn't keep living a lie, though. It wasn't fair to my parents or to me. And it certainly wasn't fair to my brother,

Connor, who I'd told after swearing him to secrecy. Plus, I was excited about opening my own beauty salon and wanted to share that joy with my family. The decision had been made: I'd tell my parents the truth at dinner tonight.

My stomach roiled. Never in a million years would my mom approve of me becoming a cosmetologist. She'd rather set her eyelash extensions on fire, watch her Cadillac Escalade do a high jump off a cliff, or trade her 5500-square foot cabin with its breathtaking views of the Rocky Mountains for a tent.

I wasn't exaggerating, either.

Actually, if my mom had things *her* complete way, I would've married my high school sweetheart, Thomas Brand IV, worked a few years at Reed Bank—which they owned outright, all three locations—popped out a couple of children and then joined my parents' country club. It took her months to recover when Tom dumped me right before high school graduation. I'd been hurt over the unexpected breakup, but ended up having to console my mom instead of the other way around.

Ever since we lost my older sister, Grace, in a terrible accident when I was young, I'd felt like I had to be twice the daughter for my parents—especially for my mom, who held my big sister in the highest regard, one that I never seemed able to reach. My stomach knotted thinking about that tragic day by the cliff, so I quickly pushed it from my mind.

In my defense, I'd tried it my mom's way most of my life in order to make her happy. But if I'd gone for my MBA like she'd pushed me to do, then something inside me would've shriveled up and died. I needed to come home and come clean. It had been eight years since I'd left for college and I couldn't stay away from my beloved hometown forever.

I'd missed Christmas Mountain.

And I'd received a sign that it was time to come home.

At the end of October, I received a letter from my school choir teacher and mentor extraordinaire, Melody King. In her own handwritten words, she'd revealed the devastating news that she was terminally ill due to a kidney cancer. I'd cried myself to sleep that night. I mean, Ms. King couldn't be more than sixty years old. Way too young to die. My eyes started to burn from imagining a world without that vibrant woman still in it.

I dabbed at the corners of my eyes, before returning both hands to the wheel. I needed to concentrate on the road or I wouldn't be arriving home shortly or anytime thereafter. But two minutes later, I felt my mind drifting back to my brave mentor.

Ms. King had always been there for me and for my besties from the middle school and high school choir teams. And if her final wish was for the seven of us to sing "I'll be Home for Christmas" together once again for her at the annual Christmas extravaganza? Well, I for one would *not* let her down.

Guilt kicked me in the chest as I thought of my besties from the choir team: Ashley, Emma, Faith, Lexi, Joy, and Carol. Even though we'd sworn to be best friends forever in our bracelet ceremony by the Falls in sixth grade, I hadn't seen any of them since we'd been arrested after high school graduation (long story). Well, Lexi and I used to keep in touch over the phone, but it had been years since I'd talked to her. That was crazy to think about. She probably thought I went into the MBA program liked I'd planned. Shudder.

I could only assume that Lexi and the rest of the team were returning to sing for Ms. King, as well. Not that I'd talked to any of them yet. I'd been too busy planning my own return. But I remembered our best friends bracelet ceremony like it was yesterday. I also remembered after graduation, I'd made a big speech to my friends about how I was going to face my mom, refuse to major in accounting, confess my real dream to her, and ask that she finally accept me for who I am rather than as a disappointing substitute for Grace.

But, nobody stood up to Ivy Reed and won.

So I'd caved like a coward.

Driving along the highway, I fingered the pink, hand-woven-out-of-string besties bracelet on my left wrist that was safely tucked under the Rolex my parents had sent me for my birthday in August. I'd vowed in sixth grade never to take this bracelet off and I never had. Even though we'd been apart for years, my friends still meant the world to me. My vision blurred as my mind flashed back to our bracelet ceremony by the waterfall.

My heart squeezed as a hot tear slipped down my cheek. I swiped it away and shook my head so hard that my dark hair fell behind my shoulders. I missed my high school besties and wished I'd kept in touch after I went off to college to get a degree in accounting (snooze). I hoped they knew that the words we'd chanted that night still held a special place in my heart.

As if feeling my pain, my SUV let out a low groan at the incline, but I figured it was more likely a reaction to not being used to these steep mountain roads. I cleared the lump in my throat and patted the dashboard. "Don't you dare die on me," I warned. "If you can handle Florida humidity and salty air then you can deal with some uphill climbs."

I hoped.

Christmas Mountain, Montana sat just over the next hill and Miami was far behind me. My heart drummed in my chest. Almost home. I'd loved Miami for many reasons—the sun, the beach, and the electrical pulse of the place—but I'd never felt rooted there.

I drove up the next rise then downward into a little dip and then the small town of Christmas Mountain spread out before me, surrounded by the Rocky Mountains. The road wandered around the side of the snow-topped mountain like a slim gray ribbon. The trees held glorious color and I spotted pines and Douglas firs. The side of the mountain towered over the road as it weaved through a series of turns until I came to a relatively flat stretch.

The downtown section of Christmas Mountain came into view and looked only slightly different despite the years that had passed. The road became a broad avenue that was separated by a center divider, which was decorated with neatly trimmed bushes. Wooden benches sat on the sidewalks and I knew if I kept driving past downtown then I'd run into the Christmas Mountain Community Center, home of the annual Christmas extravaganza where my besties and I had performed for years.

Quaint shops lined the quiet street beneath cheerful awnings. I passed the feed store, antique store, bookstore, florist, coffee shop, and more. My mouth watered as I spotted the barbecue place on my left. There's nothing in the world like good barbecue and that place made some of the best chopped pork and Brunswick stew I'd ever eaten, served with sliced bread and a sauce that would light your face on fire if you took too large a bite. Yum.

Speaking of dinner, my parents were probably wondering what had happened to me since I was running so late. But I'd be at their house shortly and then I'd tell them about my career change. My stomach clenched. Or, not.

No, I couldn't keep this secret from them any longer.

As if on cue, up on my right I spotted the former home of Coraline's Classic Beauty Salon, soon to be replaced by my very own C.M. Salon where I'd offer full hair services, manicures, pedicures, and facials. My heart rate kicked up and my gaze flew to the window of the business space I'd rented. Pride and joy hit me hard. I checked the time, sighed, and found myself pulling the SUV into a parking spot out front.

Dusk had fallen and I rationalized that my parents had better things to do on a Friday night than hold dinner for me. I definitely wanted to tell them about the salon, but it suddenly seemed better to wait until I fixed it up a bit. The more professional the salon looked when I showed my mom, the more likely she'd be at ease that I'd made the right decision.

I shot my mom a text that the trip took longer than expected, so I'd meet up with them tomorrow instead. This new plan would work much better. Plus, I should get to my friend Ruby's townhome—the place where I'd be living—at a reasonable hour. But, I mean, no harm in taking a quick peek at my business space, right?

I jumped out of the car, my feet landing on the sidewalk.

I'd played a kind of Tetris while packing my belongings into the back of my SUV and should probably get home to unpack everything, but I ignored the responsible side of my brain and hurried toward the building, my smile growing wider with each step.

Mine. All mine.

I fumbled in my purse for the keys Coraline had mailed to me after I'd leased the place from her. Then I unlocked the door. The hinges squealed, making me grimace. I had to get that fixed before opening day in two and a half weeks. I also had to put up my "coming soon" sign in the window for advertising.

But first, I needed to check out my dream space in person. I flipped on the light switch, but nothing happened. Huh. Bulb must've burned out. No matter. The streetlights from the outside sent enough light through the front window for me to look the place over.

I crossed my fingers, hoping the photos Coraline emailed me hadn't done the closed-salon justice. My gaze darted around the wide and long room, confirming the photos had indeed been accurate. Ick. I added "changing the décor" to my mental "to do" list because there was no way I could leave the scratched-up black-and-white checkered tile flooring or the orange—yes, *orange*—salon chairs in place. The heavy, old-fashioned gilt-trimmed mirrors made me chuckle, but the drooping and dusty plastic plants were certainly no laughing matter. Yikes.

I drifted through the front room to the stockroom in back, trying to envision the changes I'd make. The faint scent of disuse filled my nostrils as I eyed a shelf filled with abandoned hair products that looked like they'd escaped from the nineteen-fifties. I stared at the bottles, wondering if it would be safe to toss them into the trash or if I'd need a hazmat team to dispose of them.

Suddenly, I heard a squealing noise coming from the front of the business space. My body tensed. Had I locked the front door after I entered? I couldn't remember. This was a sweet small town, not the big city, but still. My gaze flew to the stockroom door and I listened hard. Nothing. Maybe I'd imagined the noise. I let out a breath just as a second squealing sound ensued.

The definite timbre of footsteps followed.

Oh, *no*. Someone was here.

Next came a strange high-pitched scraping sound, and goosebumps prickled up my neck. What could that be?

I squatted in a defensive stance and looked around, hoping to spot a broom or something I could use as a weapon. Coraline was an older, single woman. Surely she'd kept a baseball bat handy, right? But there weren't any makeshift weapons in sight. With no other options, I grabbed a dusty bottle of toner and uncapped it. Maybe I could toss the liquid into the intruder's eyes and blind him as I raced out. Why, oh *why*, hadn't I taken martial arts as a child?

But I refused to be killed in the stockroom of a sadly out-of-date beauty parlor. I had to make an escape. My heart pounded in my chest as I shadowed the wall and tiptoed out front, holding the toner bottle like a missile ready for launch. It was now or never.

Sucking in a deep breath, I peered around the corner into the dim room just as the lights flashed on illuminating a well-built man in cowboy boots sauntering casually toward a ladder in the center of the room. My eyes took in the tight-fitted jeans over muscular legs and the broad build beneath a gray t-shirt, with sinewy arms to boot. At least the man—intruder or not—wasn't wearing a cowboy hat or I'd have to yell, "Yee-haw!"

Instead, the toner bottle slipped from my grip and dropped against the floor, bouncing with a *thud-thud-thud*. The man's head whipped in my direction and familiar caramel-brown eyes met mine. Then the corner of the man's mouth slowly curved upward.

"Morgan Reed," he said, his low husky tone a statement and not a question.

"Dallas Parker?" I asked, my belly doing a flip. I knew that look he was giving me. It had set my heart racing back in high school and it seemed to have the same effect eight years later.

"Now we've gotten the names out of the way." He chuckled, moving away from the ladder and walking toward me. He took me in, shaking his head. "The last time I saw you it was plaid skirts and headbands. I almost didn't recognize you."

"It's me," I said, lamely. Then I glanced down at my dark-washed jeans and high-heeled black boots. Yeah, a definite outfit change from my days at Christmas Mountain High. Dallas looked different, as well. He was still tall, toned and trim, but wisdom flashed in those caramel-brown eyes now. His dark hair was much shorter these days and he looked older, but it was definitely Dallas Parker—my older brother's best friend, my secret childhood crush, and the man my mother blamed for our family's greatest tragedy. "W-What are you doing here?"

He was also the guy who had punched my boyfriend in the jaw at the end of senior year when he'd caught us making out at Kissing Bench right next to the waterfall.

"The question is what are *you* doing here?" he asked, stopping inches in front of me. "Other than dropping a bottle of . . . what is that, anyway?"

"Hair toner." I glanced at the bottle sheepishly. Then my gaze shot to the ladder in the center of the room, which I now noticed sat beneath a light fixture. He'd changed the light bulb. That was the noise I'd heard, not that of someone I needed to douse in the eyes with toner. Wait, why was Dallas changing the light bulb in my new salon? Maybe he'd become some sort of property manager, or something. "I heard a strange noise and thought you were an intruder. I guess you were just changing the light bulb in my shop."

His brows rose. "Wait a minute. Did you say *your* shop?"

"Yes," I said, my voice tight since I could see surprise written on his face. Why was he so shocked? I was perfectly capable of running my own business, thank you so much. And why did his sexy vibe affect me after all this time? So infuriating. I cleared my throat, determined not to let him see how he affected me. I picked up the bottle from the floor, dropping it into a nearby garbage can. "I'm opening my own beauty salon, so I leased this space. I assume you're the, um, property manager? Thanks for changing the light bulb for me."

"Whoa, whoa, whoa," he said, his tone suddenly condescending as he held his palms up and shook his head. "You must be in the wrong building. I'm the one who rented this place. I'm opening up a furniture store."

Chills vibrated through me. What the . . .?

Visions of opening my own beauty salon evaporated before my very eyes.

"Um, I don't think so." My hands thrust to my hips. "No way, *you* must be in the wrong place. I rented this beauty salon from Coraline of Coraline's Classic Beauty Salon and look around you, Dallas." I gestured wildly. "This is clearly a *beauty* salon, not a furniture store."

"I don't see that much beauty in it, to be honest." He looked around at the garish décor. "Those chairs are the same color as the antacid I usually drink after a plate of 'cue and slaw. Coraline clearly wanted *me* to make my mark on this place."

I sucked in a hard breath. He wasn't wrong with his antacid description, but those orange chairs were mine to use *not* his. "Let me worry about the color of my chairs."

"They aren't *your* chairs, Morgan. I rented this business space, not you."

I choked and grabbed the purse I'd dropped on a small counter next to one of the antacid-colored chairs. I dug around in it. "You must've had too much beer with your 'cue and slaw, Dallas. You didn't rent *this* place. See, I have the lease right here."

"Let me read that." He took the papers I thrust at him, his fingers brushing against mine and sending tingles up my arm. His gaze met mine as a shiver rolled through me that I hoped

The Christmas Compromise

with every fiber of my being he didn't notice. The corner of his mouth hitched up. "Missed me, huh?"

"You wish," I said, kicking myself for not having a better retort. Whatever. Anyone with eyes could tell the man was attractive. Not my body's fault for reacting that way. Not like I was going to throw my arms around him and kiss him.

Although the thought wasn't exactly unpleasant. . . .

"Maybe I do wish." His gaze simmered as I glared at him, but this only seemed to make him more amused. Finally, he unfolded the pages and scanned them. His forehead creased. Then he handed me my papers and dug around in his back pocket. "Check this out."

"What?" I asked, making sure not to let my fingers graze his as I took the papers from him. I skimmed through quickly, my heart sinking with every word. The address was correct. The dates were correct. Which meant we'd both rented the same place from Coraline. "This isn't possible."

"It's clearly possible." He shrugged and then sauntered over to a shelf sitting on the floor and resting against the wall. He picked up a hammer and began banging nails into the wood.

Was he seriously decorating *my* salon?

"Stop that," I said, marching up to him. "You can't put that shelf up in my salon."

"It's my furniture store," he retorted between hammer blows. "Look, I don't know what happened here, but my store opens in two and a half weeks and it's going to take a lot of work to get it done."

"My salon opens then, too," I said, my heart sinking. I tapped my toe against the floor as he finished hanging the shelf on the wall. "Fine, I'll use that shelf to display products. Hair gel and shampoo and conditioner."

"I'm confused." He turned to face me, the corner of his

mouth lifting. "How exactly are you opening a beauty salon? Didn't you go to school for accounting?"

Yikes! I'd been back in Christmas Mountain for all of half an hour and I was already being asked the questions I dreaded most. Wait. He knew what I'd majored in? My heart fluttered in my chest. I'd be lying if I denied the massive crush I'd had on him most of my teenage years. But I was a grown woman now and his sexy smile wouldn't work on me.

I crossed my arms. "Yes, so?"

His eyebrows rose. "Why are you opening a beauty salon if you got a degree in accounting?"

"I . . ." I dragged in a breath and then sighed. "None of your business. Okay?"

"I don't have time for this." He blew out a breath and turned away again. I couldn't help noticing how well his jeans fit. He bent over to pick up another shelf and I lost my breath. The ring of the hammer against a nail snapped me back to my senses.

"Stop hammering," I said, my fists balling at my sides. "This is my life you're playing with. My salon opens on the eighteenth of December. I've already paid for advertising and everything."

He set the hammer aside. "It's money I can't afford to lose either."

"I don't know what to do," I said, racking my brain. "I mean, clearly I need this particular space more than you do. This doesn't look anything like a furniture store. And since when did you get into furniture? I heard you were in the military."

Oh, no. His sexy smirk was back.

"You've been checking up on me, Morgan?"

I spluttered. "No. Of course not."

He gave me a wicked grin. "You sure? It sounds like you're carrying a torch for me."

"The only thing I've been carrying for you is toner, which I'd planned to throw in your face. I obviously should've done that. You're . . . a *menace*."

His brows came together. "Name one time I was a menace."

"How about the time you punched my boyfriend in the face?" I blurted.

He paused a moment and then shrugged. "He deserved it."

My jaw dropped open. "Tom was a straight-A student, a good athlete, and the entire town liked him. Maybe you were jealous."

He didn't seem the least bit perturbed by my accusation. In fact, he looked amused. "Would you have liked it if I'd been jealous?"

"No, of course not." Well, maybe a little.

"I'd like to say this has been fun, but the scowl on your face tells me you don't feel the same way. But I can't afford to delay fixing up my furniture store. So, you'll have to scowl at me while I work."

"You're impossible," I said, as he turned his back to me again. What was he doing opening a furniture store, anyway? Well, that actually did make sense considering he and most of the men in his family had worked in the sawmill until that terrible incident happened with his uncle. I pushed that out of my mind, though. "You can't open your furniture store *here*."

He faced me again, letting out an audible breath.

"Well?" I asked. Then we stood there staring at each other for what had to be several minutes. I wasn't going to budge on my dream, but I was beginning to feel exhausted.

"It's late." He pulled a cell phone out of his pocket and

checked the time. "But this is Coraline's mix-up, so we'd better just call her and she can sort this out."

"Good idea." I hoped she'd side with me once she realized the mistake. Taking the lead so she'd hear my voice first, I whipped out my own cell phone, tapped on her phone number, and then turned on the speaker. The phone rang and I held my breath as we waited for her to pick up.

A *click* sounded. "This is Coraline. I'm sorry I can't take your call, but I'm retired now and on the adventure of a lifetime. An African safari. Feel free to leave a message. I'll be back in town Christmas Eve. Cheers!"

This was *not* good.

I glanced at Dallas. He looked back at me.

"There has to be some solution here," I said, biting my lip.

He raked his hand through his hair. "I can think of one."

"You're willing to concede and leave me to my salon?" I laced my hands in prayer position, put on my cutest smile, and nodded my head causing my hair to fall against my cheek.

"Not going to happen." He shook his head, reaching out and tucking my hair behind my ear. His fingers grazed my jawline, leaving a wake of tingles along my sensitive skin. Then the corners of his mouth curved upward. "We're going to have to compromise and share the space for now."

"We are?" I asked, watching him nod. I wanted to disagree, but with Coraline gone until Christmas Eve the obvious solution was to open our businesses together. I'd just have to ignore his sexy smile and make some rules, like no tucking my hair behind my ear.

Then on Christmas Eve, one of us would get the boot.

CHAPTER TWO

I left the salon late that evening and then drove through a set of stone gates and up a short hill to the address of Ruby's townhome. I parked in front of a brick building with white windows that overlooked a small, snow-filled front yard. After that encounter with Dallas, I needed a friendly face.

I'd no sooner cut off the engine than the townhome's front door flew open and Ruby Curtis came running out. Her blonde hair was pulled up into a high ponytail and she wore a blue sweater, jeans, and boots. Her pretty face and blue eyes lit up as she hurried to where I was getting out of the driver's side and then pulled me into a welcoming hug.

Ruby and I had been friends since elementary school. She was just as dear to me as my besties from the choir team with whom I'd exchanged the bff bracelets. Ruby had been two years ahead of us in school and had been in Dallas and my brother Connor's grade. Her parents, Randall and Betty Curtis, owned the Sugar Plum Inn—a bed and breakfast near the Falls, which had been around forever.

Ruby's parents' first real date was to The Nutcracker ballet and her mom loved the Dance of the Sugar Plum Fairy. Since that night, her dad nicknamed his wife his "sugar plum fairy" and insisted on the name for the inn. So sweet.

"You're finally here!" Ruby squealed into my ear. "I was getting worried, but figured you'd stopped off to see your folks."

"Actually, I stopped by the salon," I said, hugging her hard as a feeling of dread fell over me from thinking about the lease mix-up with Dallas. I fought to shake it off.

Ruby released me and we stood there smiling at each other. Finally, she reached for the bag I held. "Let me help you with that . . . *wow*." She gestured toward my SUV and the stacks of boxes inside. "You fit all of that in there?"

I gave her a rueful grin. "Yeah, I'm terrified that if I remove one thing then all of my stuff will come flying out."

She threw her head back and laughed. "Like that time we opened the closet door in the prop room at Christmas Mountain High?"

"I've missed you." I laughed at her story and hugged her again. "And I remember how we almost quit the drama club over the chaos caused by that prop room closet. Nothing like getting buried in an avalanche of wigs and old makeup."

Ruby squeezed me back. "It's good to have you home again. I worried we'd never get you out of Florida. Although I did have a fun time visiting you there." She stepped back, her gaze scanning me. "Those boots are gorgeous and you look amazing. Nobody's going to recognize you from your high school days."

"I'm looking forward to catching up with old friends," I said, wondering what they would think of my new look. When I'd left Christmas Mountain, I'd been doing my best to live up to the perfect good girl image and expectations my mom had for me. It had been all plaid skirts, pressed white blouses, and headbands. I never would've worn black boots with a heel, tight jeans, or the now-standard pop of fuchsia on my lips. "How are your parents doing?" I asked.

"Same as always. They eat, sleep, and breathe the inn. Bookings have been slower these days due to the decrease in tourism, but the bed and breakfast is doing well enough."

"Glad to hear it," I said, my stomach growling. My cheeks heated and I put a hand over my belly. "Sorry, I forgot to stop for dinner."

She chewed at her bottom lip. "Maybe we should relax before unpacking then. Want a sandwich?"

"Yes, please," I said, following Ruby inside her townhome.

The kitchen and living room were an open concept and Ruby's personality was stamped everywhere. Vases on small tables held fresh flowers. There were antique rugs on the hardwood floors. Paintings of mountains hung on the walls next to those incredible windows. The kitchen countertops were granite, accented by a subway tile backsplash and stainless steel appliances.

Ruby went to the stovetop. "I'd just finished making this grilled cheese when you pulled up. We can split it. You still like tomato basil soup, I hope?"

"I do." I smiled, loving that my friend knew me so well.

"Would you like some iced tea?"

I lifted an eyebrow. "Is it sweet?"

"Oh, no." She paused in the act of ladling soup from the stove into oversized bowls that I recognized as her grandmother's Spode. "I forgot you're a Southerner."

I blinked at her. "Come again?"

"You lived in the South, so you probably don't drink plain iced tea anymore."

"I love iced tea," I said, dropping onto a barstool.

She set a steaming bowl and a plate on the counter in front of me. "Not that Florida is totally the South. It's Florida."

I groaned inwardly. The argument over whether or not Florida's part of the South had been raging for decades. "Either way, I still drink plain, unsweetened iced tea."

"Good," she said, hurrying to the fridge and pulling out a white pitcher. She filled two glasses with ice, poured our tea, and then took a seat next to me.

I scooped up a spoonful of soup, which smelled delicious. "Mmm."

"Made it from scratch," she said, fiddling with her napkin for a minute. "You tell your mom about the salon yet?"

I shifted on the stool. "Um . . ."

She sighed, spooning up some soup. "Morgan, she's going to be hurt that you didn't tell her."

"I'm trying to avoid her getting hurt." I squirmed. I hadn't told my parents I was moving in with Ruby, either, but that was the least of what they would be upset about. "You know how controlling my mom can be. I think she'll take the news better if I get the salon set up first in a way she'd approve of." I sighed. "She might talk me out of my dream if I'm not careful to present it the right way at the right time."

My friend gave me a sympathetic smile. "Your secret is always safe with me."

"Thanks." I sipped the iced tea, wanting to change the subject. "Unfortunately, I have bigger worries right now than my mom being upset with me."

"Like what?" she asked.

I swallowed a bite of sandwich. "You won't believe what happened when I stopped by to check out the business space I rented."

She dipped her spoon into the bowl. "Don't tell me the ceiling caved in. That place has been empty for months."

"Worse," I said, dabbing my mouth with the napkin.

"What's worse than a caved-in ceiling?"

"Dallas Parker," I said, flatly.

She choked on the tea she'd been drinking. "Sorry, not what I'd been expecting you to say. Dallas, huh? What gives? I knew he'd moved back in town, but I haven't seen him."

I lifted the spoon for my soup and groaned. "He has a lease for the same business space I rented for my beauty salon."

She blinked. "I'm confused."

"Me, too." I stirred my soup slowly. "It turns out that Coraline, the landlady, somehow made a mistake and rented the business space to both of us."

Ruby gripped the edge of the island like she was afraid she'd topple off the stool otherwise. "She rented the same space to both of you? No way."

"Yes way." I nodded, scooping up more of the delicious soup.

She shook her head. "What on earth could Dallas possibly want with a beauty salon?"

"His plan is to turn Coraline's Classic Beauty Salon into a furniture store." I squeezed the spoon in my hand and then tapped it relentlessly against the counter with a *tink-tink-tink*. "Can you believe he won't give up the business space? I thought he'd joined the Marines."

"Don't take your frustration out on the silverware." She took the spoon from me, set it down on the countertop, and patted the handle. "See? All better now."

I threw her a look. "You're not helping."

She chewed her fingernail thoughtfully. "Dallas did leave for the Marines after high school, but he's been back in Christmas Mountain almost a year. Bought a place with some acreage outside of town. Keeps to himself, so I don't hear much about him. Furniture store, huh?"

"That's what he said." I took the last bite of my sandwich, chewing slowly. "I mean, clearly the space won't work for his needs. It's set up as a beauty salon. For my purposes, I only need to give the place a facelift. I've already paid for advertising and my salon opens in two and a half weeks. I can't afford the time arguing with him about who deserves the space more, because there's so much I have to do before opening day. The salon chairs are orange. Need I say more?"

"Like a perky orange or an antacid color?"

"Antacid." I groaned, tucking my chin to my chest. "I know this leasing situation isn't Dallas's fault, but my salon is currently orange. Oh, *so* orange . . ."

"The orange!" Ruby threw her palms up, and then burst out laughing. "Don't you remember when our moms took us to Coraline's that time the upscale salon was booked and we had to have our hair done for the school drama production? I almost went blind in that place."

Despite everything I burst into laughter. "Yes, I remember having our hair done there. I don't remember the orange being so overwhelming."

She leaned in closer. "How is Dallas going to sell furniture in an orange-colored beauty salon?"

"Right?" I nodded, finishing the last of my soup. "It looks like someone froze the nineteen-fifties in there."

"You need to call your landlady," she said, stacking our empty plates and bowls before taking them to the sink.

My shoulders slumped. "We tried. She's out of town and on a safari until Christmas Eve."

"Really?" Ruby's eyebrows went up. "That's amazing. I mean, that's a once in a lifetime adventure right there. I wonder where she's on safari?"

"Somewhere in Africa," I said, remembering how Ruby had always wanted to travel. "Do you know what Dallas suggested? He said we should share the space and open our businesses together."

She rinsed the dishes and then put them in the dishwasher. "Is the space big enough for both businesses?"

"It's a big place," I said, remembering the layout. "But I can't have him hammering nails while my clients are getting their hair done. Or having a facial. A salon is supposed to be relaxing. I spent extra time and tuition money to become a fully licensed esthetician, hair stylist, and nail technician. A furniture store and a beauty salon don't mix."

Ruby nodded. "You're right. That's *way* worse than a caved in ceiling."

I dropped my head in my hands. "What am I going to do? There is no other appropriate space available for rent. Plus, I already purchased ads from the *Christmas Mountain Herald* as well as online ads. I paid for my own website and even social media pages are ready to launch for my grand opening. On top of this, I still have to deal with my parents."

Ruby clapped her hands. "I know what will cheer you up."

"The news that Dallas Parker has fled town?" I asked, watching her shake her head. It had been a long shot. "What then?"

"Guess who I heard is coming to town for Christmas?" she said, using a singsong voice.

I was so *not* in the mood for a guessing game. "Just tell me."

"I'll give you a clue." She smiled, wiggling her brows. "Someone handsome who you dated in high school and were totally gaga for . . ."

That narrowed it down to my ex, Thomas Brand IV. I hadn't been popular with boys in high school. I'd been dubbed Miss Goody Two-Shoes with good reason.

"Tom Brand?" I asked, wondering how the return of my ex who dumped me was supposed to cheer me up. Maybe for extra cheering she'd burn my favorite boots.

"Yes, Tom!" Ruby put an arm around me. "You two were so cute together when you were young love birds. Wouldn't it be sweet if you reconnected and you married your high school sweetheart? I heard he's landed some high-salaried job. Why did you two break up again?"

"He dumped me," I said, my voice deadpan. "Right after Dallas Parker punched him in the face." Suddenly, I pictured Dallas and his sexy smile. Shiver. I shook my head, trying to chase the vision of Dallas that kept lingering in my head. "Ah, getting dumped. Thanks for the walk down memory lane. I'm totally cheered up now."

"I'm sorry for bringing up Tom." Ruby patted my shoulder, clearly not getting that I was upset about the fact that I was mentally drooling over my nemesis, not because Tom dumped me eight years ago. "I didn't mean to bring up something painful," she said.

I waved my hand dismissively. "Tom was a long time ago. I'm way over him."

"Dallas really punched him in the face?" she asked.

I nodded. "When he caught us making out on the Kissing Bench at the Falls."

Ruby's eyes went round and wide. "No."

"Yes." I twisted my fingers together. "Dallas ruined my relationship and now he's ruining my life again. Tom never really said why he wanted to break up with me, but I think he was scared Dallas would sock him again."

"Why would Dallas do that?" Ruby watched me shrug, and then she shook her head. "Dallas has always had a bit of a bad boy reputation. But we had a lot of fun with him in our younger years. And he's your brother's best friend."

"We did have good times," I said, remembering how Ruby, Dallas, Connor, and I would hang out and go for adventure walks. But that was before my mom blamed him for the accident that cost Grace her life. I shook my head to clear the thought. "I don't know what to do about the salon, Ruby. Dallas has a signed lease and so I can't throw him out."

"Not unless he *wanted* out," she said.

An idea hit. "Wait a minute. . . His furniture store will probably be super manly right? Like him?" I rolled my eyes, unable to believe I'd just said that aloud. I plunged onward. "What if I make it hard for him to *want* to be there? I can decorate the beauty salon super feminine, so he'd want to find a new space. I mean, men don't usually want to be anywhere near a beauty salon anyway, right?"

She raised a shoulder. "I'm sure that's true. I can't picture your brother wanting to hang out at your salon for a mani/pedi."

"Right?" I laughed, making a mental note to let my brother know I'd arrived in town.

Ruby's phone beeped from where it sat on the counter, plugged into the USB port. She lifted her phone, checked the screen, and groaned. "Work email coming through. I set up an alert on my phone. It's late, so it must be important. I'd better check the email."

I felt a pang of guilt. "I haven't even asked how you like your new career."

"I never thought I'd own a doggie spa and training business, but I love it. Keeps me busy practically twenty-four-seven, though," she said, holding her phone up as evidence to her statement.

"You were always good with animals growing up and always dragging in some stray as I recall," I said, looking around the kitchen. "I'm surprised you don't have a house full."

"I would if I could but this is a rental with a no-pet policy in place." She muttered as she checked her email on her phone. "I hate to leave you with the SUV to be unpacked, but I have to call my manager at the kennel. He's having an issue and wants to get my take on it. Apparently some dog needs an obedience and manners class."

"Maybe I should send Dallas over to you for some lessons in manners," I joked, thinking of how he'd tucked my hair behind my ear without asking. Not that I'd hated it, exactly.

She giggled. "Or an aggression class, since he punched your boyfriend in the face for no reason. Speaking of. . . I wonder what made him do that. Maybe he had a crush on you and wanted you all to himself."

"I doubt it," I said, remembering Dallas never had trouble getting dates.

"Just saying that I wouldn't be surprised." She gave me a knowing look. "Anyway, I'll come help you unpack when I'm done with the call. Glad to have you home."

"Thanks, Ruby," I said, wishing my arrival home had gone more smoothly. With the luck I was having, next I'd probably get a concussion from falling boxes in my SUV. Maybe if I had a serious injury then Dallas would feel sorry for me and let me have my salon space back.

As I walked out the front door, I pictured myself with a white bandage around my head, staring up at Dallas pathetically, trying to appeal to his sensitive side. An image of those caramel-brown eyes looking down at me with concern made my belly flutter. I imagined him tucking a lock of my hair behind my ear, his fingers running along my jawline before he pressed his lips to my forehead. My chest warmed and I could see myself lifting my mouth to his. . . .

Suddenly, my foot caught in front of the other one on the icy pathway and I found myself falling face-first onto the front lawn. I landed with a "Harrumph!" The moisture from the dew-covered grass began seeping into the front of my pants in a very cold way, thanks to it being December and all. I inhaled the earthy scent, before lifting my nose from the ground.

This had to be the universe's way of telling me to stop thinking about Dallas Parker. That would be hard to do if we were sharing the same business space. Maybe he would leave if I took my idea and started "beautifying" the place in a big feminine way. If I didn't want to fall on my face again, it was certainly worth a try.

CHAPTER THREE

The next morning, I had breakfast with Ruby before she went to work. Then I spent the rest of the morning unpacking and catching up on paperwork for my new business. Later that afternoon, I drove into town, which was buzzing with people on the sidewalks.

    I pulled into a parking space a few doors down from the salon and got out, ducking my head as I spotted a couple standing near one of the old-fashioned style lamps that ran along the sidewalks. The man and the woman each held a wreath in their hands, making it look like they were about to start decorating downtown for Christmas.

    I didn't recognize the couple, but you never knew who knew whom in this town and I didn't want anyone to tell my mom they'd seen me downtown. I'd shamefully texted her this morning, making up an excuse as to why I couldn't meet my parents for breakfast at Prancer's Pancake House. Guilt seeped over me, but I needed to improve my salon to increase my odds of a favorable outcome when I told them my plan. If they saw I had the potential for a capable business, then hopefully they'd support my decision to change careers.

I strode past the couple on the sidewalk and the wind kicked up a chill as I rushed toward the door, key already in hand. I'd just turned the key in the lock when I heard a familiar female voice call out, "Morgan Reed? Is that you? Yes, it is you, Morgan."

Oh, *no*. I flinched, recognizing that nasally voice even though I hadn't heard it in eight years. I steeled my nerves, plastering on what I hoped passed for a smile and not a grimace as I turned to face Addie Wilcox.

Addie was the mother of a girl my brother had dated back in high school. She was also a major gossip and everyone in town knew it, which was why her cocktail parties were always packed. She rushed toward me with a large wreath in her hands and a curious look on her face.

"Mrs. Wilcox, nice to see you," I lied. My teeth clamped together as Addie puffed to a halt and surveyed my old jeans, thickly soled shoes, and dark hoodie before her eyes flicked upward to my long, dark hair, which I'd put up in a messy knot since I planned to be cleaning all day. "Are you on the town's Christmas decorating committee this year?" I asked, hoping to divert her from asking questions about me.

"Spreading cheer, as always," she said, glancing from me to where I'd been heading. The woman was way too astute. "What on earth could you be doing at Coraline's Classic Beauty Salon? I mean . . ." Her gaze drifted up to my hair and she made a clucking noise. "I can see why you would come here but, honey, Coraline's is closed. She's been retired for months. She's on an African Safari until Christmas, which . . . good for her! She could use a break being a single woman at *her* age."

"Huh." My brain screamed to *run, run fast, run anywhere else but here*. The last thing I needed was Addie Wilcox knowing anything about my salon, because if she found out then everyone in town would know. "I . . . *love* your hair, Mrs. Wilcox. It's so well kept."

"Thank you, honey." She patted her Farrah Fawcett 'do, which looked a bit too heavily hair-sprayed. "Your mom was over at the country club last week, but I don't recall her saying anything about you coming back to town for the holidays."

"Er . . ." I floundered for a moment and my horror escalated when a black truck pulled to a halt in the recently vacated space in front of the salon.

Dallas got out of the driver's side looking unnervingly hot in a dark brown leather jacket. My belly flipped and I started to sweat. He didn't seem to notice Addie or me on the sidewalk. He just walked around to the back of the truck, let the tailgate down, took some monstrous contraption out, and then started carrying it toward the front door of the salon.

Addie nudged my arm. "Isn't that Dallas Parker?"

"Yes, I believe so," I said, desperately hoping he didn't look this way. What if he told Addie I was opening a beauty salon? My parents would be so hurt if I didn't tell them first and I would be totally to blame. My gut clenched.

Addie shifted the wreath in her arms. "I knew he moved back to Christmas Mountain. Word is he's been hiding out in that cabin he purchased outside of town."

Um, not so accurate. He wasn't hiding out. I only wished he were in hiding right now. Instead of heading straight my way. I had to do something. I grabbed Addie's wreath from her hands and ducked behind it. "This wreath is lovely. And I adore this scent," I said, shoving my nose into the pine needles and inhaling, hoping to hide my face.

"Yes, well, I'd better get back to decorating." Addie squinted around the wreath, giving me a weird look before pulling it away from me as Dallas approached. Addie leaned toward me. "Hey, I believe your folks are having dinner at The

Chop House tonight. I'll be dining there as well. Maybe I'll stop by their table to let them know how good it's been to run into you," she said.

"Lovely to see you, too." My stomach knotted. I needed to call my brother fast. If anyone could get Mom and Dad to agree to have dinner somewhere else it would be him. Dallas stepped onto the sidewalk. The thing he carried appeared heavy and his thick leather jacket showed off the strength in his arms as he toted the contraption.

I had the wildest thought just then. A man carrying that load would probably be able to tote me pretty easily, too. Maybe toss me over his shoulder and walk right off with me.

My face heated and my pulse raced alarmingly fast. No! This was my nemesis. I shouldn't have hot thoughts about him. What was happening to me?

Dallas set the contraption down on the sidewalk and pushed it toward the front door, next to where Addie and I stood.

He glanced at us for the first time and his mouth stretched into a smile. "Good morning, Morgan. Would you hold the door open for me?"

I glanced at Addie, who was watching with avid eyes. "Sure, Dallas. Nice to see you again," I said, cringing at the strange look he gave me. Groaning inwardly, I yanked the door open and he entered my salon, giving me another odd look.

To my relief, someone called for Addie to hurry up with that wreath and she dashed off with a quick goodbye. I waited until she'd turned her head, then I pulled the door of the salon back open and slipped inside in time to see Dallas plugging the machine he'd brought into an outlet.

I strode over to him. "What do you think you're doing? What is that thing?"

"It's to take the tile up." He gave me a grin and I noticed

he'd removed his jacket, revealing one of those tee shirts that showed off his well-defined arms. *Wowzers.* "Unless, of course, you enjoy the antique diner ambience and want that tile left on your half of the floor," he said.

"Not exactly," I admitted. But I didn't want him to do a single thing to my floor except cross it on his way back out the door. "I doubt the landlady will let us uproot the tile."

"She gave me permission in my lease. I can make any necessary repairs and remodels as long as I pay for them. I don't have the funds to hire someone to take up the floor, or lay another one, and no way am I willing to live with this." His gaze flew to the scratched up black and white checkered floor, before looking back at me quickly. I couldn't blame him for looking away fast. That tile was enough to make any person dizzy.

"Okay, you have a point. The tile is terrible," I agreed. And now that I thought about it, I had that provision in my lease as well. I couldn't let him put in a new floor before I ousted him from my space, though. Then I'd owe him a big chunk of money. "I can help renovate and do an equal share. How about if I clean and take down those mirrors?"

"With what I'm doing, everything would be dirty again right away. Cleaning now won't do us any good."

"Oh." I gulped, my belly doing a flip at the way he'd said "us." I needed to get a hold of myself. He was just a man after all. . . Make that a very sexy man, who was handling heavy machinery with ease. Shiver.

"Should we even keep those mirrors?" He leaned in close to me as he eyed them.

My breath caught in my throat. My entire body went taut as his fingers brushed mine. I felt tingles along my skin, making me wonder what his entire hand would feel like against my flesh. Not a good thought, Morgan. I had to get away.

I stepped back so fast my feet tangled together and I fell backward into an orange chair. When my bottom hit the seat, a large cloud of dust puffed up around me, making me cough. I wiggled my nose as tickles wound inside my nostrils until I finally sneezed hard. How embarrassing.

"You all right?" He held out his hand, pulled me to my feet, and then glanced at our entwined fingers. He lifted his gaze to me. "You must've gotten too close to Addie's wreath."

"I guess so." I reluctantly removed my hand from his—even though it had felt warm and cozy there—and then rubbed my nose. Addie Wilcox and her wreath. First, she'd made me worry about her telling my mom where I was and now her wreath had set off my allergies. So much for her claim of spreading good cheer as she decorated for Christmas. "I'll get my supplies from the SUV," I said, dusting myself off.

I started toward the door, doing my best to act dignified after my fall into the antacid-colored chair. I caught a glimpse of myself in a mirror and groaned. It was hard to be dignified when you have massive dust on your booty.

I went to the car and fetched the cleaning supplies I'd brought with me, keeping one eye out for Addie the whole time. The decorating crew had moved further down the street toward the town square, but there was no guarantee she wouldn't see me. The woman had eyes like a hawk. I held the box up high to hide my face as I went back into the salon.

Remembering Addie's comment about The Chop House, I set the things down, whipped out my cell, and dialed my brother's number. No answer. I decided not to leave a message. This situation was way too complicated and I needed to hash it out with him. I tucked the phone into my pocket and saw Dallas fiddling with the tile-removing machine.

I moved out of the way as he reached for a button. The machine came on with a loud rumble. "How long is this going to take?" I asked.

"Hours," he shouted back.

Great. What should I do? Deciding I should salvage the mirrors, I used a screwdriver to remove the old-fashioned frames from the wall. Pieces of the sheetrock crumbled as I removed the mirror. I released a long breath as I realized I'd have to patch the large screw holes. Then I could paint the walls in a neutral color.

The machine behind me whirred and whined, a thin and high sound that set my teeth on edge. I still wasn't sure we should keep the mirrors, but I couldn't just stand there while he was working. I bent to check out the base of the orange chairs. They seemed fine. But what did I know? It's not like they needed a cut and color, something I was actually qualified for. Maybe I could replace the top portions of the chairs. That would save both money and time since they looked like they still functioned fine.

I gave the foot lever an experimental press. The chair came upward with a harsh grating sound and suddenly started spinning like a top.

I shrieked and fell back, holding the screwdriver out like it would somehow ward off disaster. But the chair only spun faster. A pair of hands came from behind me, drawing me back up against a hard and lean body. With my heart pounding, it took me a minute to realize my back rested against Dallas's chest.

"What did you do?" he asked, his mouth pressed beside my ear.

"I-I just tapped it," I said, flushed. I'd pressed the foot lever and now I was pressed against Dallas's body with his hands gripping my arms. Was it hot in here?

He pulled me away from the chair, which was whirling faster than ever. "Any idea how to turn it off?"

I glanced down at the foot lever. "The lever?"

He released me and I brought my hand to my forehead, feeling dizzy from the interaction. Dallas rushed forward, stomping down on the lever. The chair stopped spinning and I exhaled in relief. That relief was short-lived when the chair started sliding up and down, whining loudly as ominous black smoke puffed out of the base. Uh-oh.

I stared at the orange chair in horror. This was way worse than acid indigestion. I was so sure that the entire salon was about to go up in a literal puff of smoke that I couldn't even move.

With a high-pitched whine, the machine startlingly cut off with a loud *crack* and *pop* and then the lights went out. All was suddenly quiet.

Dallas turned to me, his eyebrows rising. "I think the chair is protesting its color."

I appreciated he was trying to make a joke to ease the mood since I felt beyond humiliated. I was supposed to be helping, not causing chairs to freak out. "What can I do?" I asked.

"Don't worry about it." He touched my arm, giving me a reassuring smile. "Let me check the breaker box to see what's going on."

He strode to the back room, his legs clad in those tight jeans and I followed, watching him open a metal box on the wall. His eyes narrowed in concentration and there was dirt smudged on his left cheek. He looked all rugged and insanely sexy. My heart threatened to jump right out of my chest as he leaned against the wall, his shirt tightening along his upper body. Yum.

"This is not good," he said.

I had to agree. I mean, I was ogling him like he was a Dutch baby, one of those delicious pastries they sold over at the barbecue place and which I never could resist. Gulp.

"What do you mean?" I asked, my voice unsteady.

"I reset the breaker but it keeps popping. Probably a short-circuit. We need to get an electrician to look at this."

Anxiety hit me like a freight train. "How long before the power can be turned back on?"

He began flipping switches. "Depends on how fast someone can come out. I'll make a call. Everything I need to do requires power. If an electrician isn't available then there won't be anything more to do in here today."

"I'm sorry." I didn't want to admit it but he was right. I sighed. My toe kicked across the floor. An idea came and I brightened. "I could take the chairs out without the power on, but I'm sort of afraid to touch them now."

"It's a good idea to get those things out now, especially if the wiring to them is potentially dangerous. I'll grab my tools after I call about the breaker box." He sauntered toward the door, looking confident and unperturbed about the huge mess I'd made. He tried several electricians, confirming nobody was available this late on a Saturday. Luckily, he booked someone for tomorrow but the guy was charging us double for a Sunday.

Determined to fix my own mess, I raced to a chair—not the one that went wild on me—and knelt down by the base. I stuck the screwdriver into a screw and began to twist. It didn't move. Argh! The screw seemed to have rusted into place. I grunted, pushing down with all my strength. But, nothing.

Dallas's boots appeared before me. "I have power tools."

I glanced up at him, biting my lip. "There's no power."

"They run on battery packs." He grinned, kneeling down beside me. "Let me help you."

"No, I've almost got it," I lied, wanting to be able to fix the problem myself. Sweat popped across my forehead as I bent to work the screw again, holding my breath as I tried to get it to turn even a millimeter. Finally, I withdrew. "Okay, have at it."

He stuck the drill into a screw, hit a button, and the screw whirled up easy as pie.

"Thank you," I said, giving him a weary smile. I held the bases in place as he got the screws out and cut the wires off the bases so they could be hauled out.

As we worked together, I found his head close to mine as he attempted to free a stubborn screw. I glanced at him. Not only was he sweet, helpful, and capable, he was also hot. So insanely hot. He always had been. Back when I was a teen, I'd had many dreams fantasizing about the two of us being together. But knowing my mom blamed him for Grace's death made it hard for me to hang out with him after the accident. I'd never blamed Dallas, but I didn't want to betray my mom. Connor never took sides, but he wasn't the only living daughter.

The last screw came out and he helped me hold the base up as I made it to my feet. The salon was growing darker by the second and I shot a look at the windows. I hadn't realized how much time had passed while we'd been working.

"I think that's all that can be done today," he said.

I nodded, tearing my eyes away from the window. "I agree." My worries came flooding back. This latest development didn't bode well. Neither did Addie spotting me.

"So, how about dinner?" he asked, brushing his hands on the front of his jeans.

My belly flipped. "You mean like a date?"

"Would you like it to be a date?"

Yes. "No."

"Well, let's just call it dinner then. I need to eat. You need to eat. Let's go together."

"I don't know . . ." I glanced around at the space. I still needed to convince him to let me have this space for my salon. But I felt way too tempted to say yes. Although, rationally, I probably could find out what might make him change venues if I brought it up in a casual dinner conversation.

"It's just dinner, Morgan. I'll take you for barbecue and get you a Dutch baby for dessert."

I opened my mouth to protest, but I could envision the pile of chopped meat with a sweet and spicy sauce and some slaw on the side . . . and those Dutch babies. If I said yes, it was only for the business. So I could feel him out to get an idea of what might drive him absolutely crazy so he'd want to find a new space.

I took a deep breath. "Okay, it's a date. I mean dinner."

It was just dinner. Unfortunately, I was already looking way too forward to it.

CHAPTER FOUR

"Am I out of my mind?" I asked my reflection in the bathroom mirror. "I must be," I said, letting out a sigh as I brushed my hair and then tossed it over my shoulders.

I struck a pose, throwing a flirty smile at the mirror. My smile was so wide it showed every tooth and a lot of gums. Not exactly sexy. How long had it been since I'd gone on a date? Too long. The last guy I'd dated had been a client from the salon in Miami. We went on a few dates, decided we didn't have much in common, and then we both moved on. For me, dating had always been so *blah*.

Not that dinner with Dallas was a real date, I reminded myself.

I applied my favorite fuchsia color to my lips and then practiced a toned down smile in the mirror. Less scary. Much better. I dressed in a red sweater with a boat neck, black slacks, and my favorite black boots with their sharp heels.

Finally ready, I stepped back from the mirror just as the doorbell rang. Thank goodness Ruby was still at work. She'd probably be thrilled I was going to dinner with Dallas and she might read more into it than was there. She was such a romantic, but this was only a business dinner. I grabbed my purse and headed for the door.

I swung the front door open and my belly did a flip. Dallas stood there, dressed in dark slacks and a long-sleeve button-down shirt. He wore his leather jacket and he'd taken the time to shave. The scent of his aftershave drifted toward me on a breeze of cool air and I inhaled the woodsy and masculine scent that was all Dallas.

Our gazes connected and locked. Shiver.

"You look beautiful," he said, his voice low.

"You don't look bad yourself," I said, keeping my answer brief so I wouldn't blurt out how well those clothes fit him or how that jacket brought out the caramel color in his brown eyes. My legs turned to cooked spaghetti and I fought to regain composure.

"Shall we go?" He stepped aside, putting his hand on the small of my back as I fell into step beside him and we walked down the front path toward his truck.

He opened the passenger door for me, making butterflies go crazy in my belly. Such a gentleman. Not a date, I reminded myself.

He hopped in the driver's side, cranked the engine and then we set off.

I glanced out the window at the surrounding mountains. "I love how the snow looks like powdered sugar on the mountain tops."

He nodded. "You didn't get much winter in Florida."

"No." I smiled, peering out at the winter beauty with delight. "Hurricanes? Yes. Snow? Unfortunately not."

"Miami, right?"

"Yes." I nodded, my brows coming together when he made a right turn, instead of heading downtown as I'd expected. "The barbecue place is the other direction."

He chuckled. "I know, but we're too dressed up for 'cue and slaw. I'm taking you somewhere nicer."

"Nicer?" I asked, biting my lip. That sounded way too sweet and the last thing I wanted was for this to be like a *real* date. I squirmed but decided it was fine. I had that plan and I needed to carry it out, *pronto*.

He took a hard right turn and we headed up a hill. I opened my mouth to comment on the pretty Christmas lights on the houses but then suddenly realized where we were headed. Dallas pulled into the parking lot of The Chop House, the same restaurant where Addie Wilcox said my folks were supposed to have dinner tonight.

That was when it hit me that I'd completely forgotten to call my brother again. Being around Dallas was way too distracting and he'd already gotten out of the truck and opened my door.

I gawked at him. "Um, I didn't expect to come here."

"You used to like the unexpected as I recall." He reached for my hand and before I even knew what was happening my boots were on the ground.

His touch sent warm flares streaking up and down my body and to complicate matters he was standing so close to me that his aftershave filled my senses again and I forgot to protest. He kept my hand in his, guiding me toward the door in a gentlemanly fashion.

My gaze shot around the parking lot but didn't see my parents' car. I breathed a bit easier, but not much. I had no idea what time they were heading in for dinner, or if they had parked on the other side of the lot. Maybe Addie Wilcox had gotten it wrong, I reasoned.

We reached the front door, which was a carved slab of burled oak set into the recessed doorway of the restaurant. The Chop House had been modeled after a hunting lodge, but promised a fine dining experience and as we stepped in it was clear that was what they delivered.

The foyer was expensively tiled. Small leather sofas and deep chairs were in casual groupings, inviting those who had to wait to take a seat. The smell of leather combined with the scent of food and the perfume and cologne of the people ahead of us in the short line.

As we waited, Dallas kept hold of my hand, which I liked way too much. To distract myself, I looked upward, taking in the high, beamed ceilings. The host station looked hand-carved from some rich, deep wood and was set up to look like a reception desk at a high-end hotel.

The hostess, an elegant woman with her blonde hair pulled up in a French twist, greeted us and checked Dallas's name off a list—telling me he'd called ahead and that the change to a nice restaurant had most definitely not been spontaneous—and then she led us through the restaurant.

My heart did a triple flip in my chest when I saw Addie, and a bunch of her equally gossipy cronies, seated at a table near the stone fireplace. I veered to the other side of Dallas, who squeezed my hand as he blinked in confusion.

I gave him a sheepish grin.

He lifted an eyebrow but didn't ask. Thankfully.

She led us to a private table and smiled. "Your server will be with you shortly."

"Thank you." Dallas released my hand and waited for me to be seated.

I dropped into the chair, peeking over my shoulder to see Addie looking down the aisle in our direction. Dallas stood right beside me, so I wasn't sure if she could see me or not. Desperate now, I switched chairs, moving into the deepest, darkest corner as fast as possible.

Dallas slid into the seat across from me. "What's going on?"

"Nothing," I lied. My gaze traveled across the room to the table opposite the fireplace—and Addie's table—and that's when things went from bad to a whole lot of worse. My folks were there! I grabbed the menu and parked it on the right side of my face, peeking over the top of the menu toward my parents, who were chatting away. "I'm just hungry, that's all."

Dallas's finger hooked the top of my menu and pressed down. I yanked the menu back up immediately. "Tell me what's going on, Morgan."

I faked an innocent expression. "What do you mean?"

He leveled me with his eyes. "You're acting weird and Addie Wilcox is leaning way out of her chair to stare over here." His gaze traveled from me to Addie's table. "Correction. Addie has leaned so far out of her chair, she's fallen off."

I groaned. "Please tell me you're joking."

"Wish I were." He shook his head.

I peeked around the side of the menu to see Addie splayed out across the beautiful hardwood floor. One of her friends reached down to help her up. My gaze flicked to Dallas. "Did she see me?" I asked, terrified.

He opened his mouth to answer, just as a uniformed woman appeared before us, setting a leather clad wine list on the table.

"Good evening." She nodded to each of us. "I'm Emily and I'll be serving you tonight. May I interest you in a wine flight? We have a lovely trio of reds beautifully paired for steak and chops, and we also have some incredible whites, more on the dry side, that pair well with our pasta, seafood and chicken dishes."

Dallas looked at me. It hit me then that this place was shockingly expensive and he had indicated that he wasn't exactly rolling in money. Guilt hit me suddenly. He was opening a business and probably couldn't afford a nice dinner like this to boot.

I took a deep breath. "I insist on buying us a bottle, or the flights. I mean, since you offered to buy my dinner."

He shook his head. "Nope. This is all me."

Emily clasped her hands in front of her. "Would you like some time to look over the wine menu?"

Dallas glanced at me. "Want me to choose a red?"

"Sounds good," I said, my nerves on edge.

He ordered a bottle and then coughed into his hand. "Ahem, red alert."

I tucked my chin, wondering if he was making some kind of wine joke. If so, I didn't get it. "Have you taken any medication? You shouldn't mix that with alcohol, you know."

He flared his eyes and tilted his head in the direction of the fireplace. "No, red alert. As in, Addie Wilcox is heading this way."

"What . . .?" I gasped and then did the first thing that came to mind. I dove beneath the table. My cheek pressed against Dallas's well-muscled calf for a second and then I scooted backward on the floor, trying to stay as deep into the shadows as possible.

"Dallas Parker." Addie's nasally voice drifted from above. "How good to see you. Didn't I see a woman come into the restaurant with you?"

I held my breath.

"Good evening," Dallas said, and then there was a long pause. "No *date* for me tonight. Even if I wished I were on a *date*, I just have to settle with dinner."

I seriously considered biting his leg to halt his over-the-top performance. And was he emphasizing the word date for my benefit? Of course we couldn't be on a real date when we'd been unwillingly thrown together in that business space, and sharing a business space with Dallas Parker was going to freak my mom out enough. She'd probably keel over if I were dating him. I had to give Dallas props for answering Addie's question without lying, though. *Bravo.*

Addie shifted on her feet. "I must be getting old and my eyes must be playing tricks on me because I could have sworn I saw you come in with a woman, but it was too dark to see who she was . . ."

"No date for me. Alas."

Alas? *Really?*

I peered at Addie's feet, which were solidly planted on the floor and soon joined by a pair of super cute black heels.

"Should I pour a glass for you and the lady, sir?" Emily's voice rang out.

I bit my lip, since she'd just given me away. I stared at the fringe of tablecloth, waiting for Addie to pull it back and yell, "Aha!"

Stressed? Me? Maybe a little.

"Yes," Dallas said, clearing his throat. "A glass for me and another for Addie Wilcox, the lovely lady who visited lonesome me at my table."

Oh, man. I was *so* going to owe Dallas big time if we pulled this off.

"Handsome lonesome you, Dallas," Addie said, giggling. "I might have a friend's daughter to introduce you to . . ."

Dallas coughed loudly then nudged my shoulder with his knee. I nudged him back, jealousy flooding over me as I awaited his answer.

"I'm not a blind date kind of guy," he finally said.

"Well, maybe I'll just have to stage a chance meeting then," Addie said, then laughed profusely as if she'd told the funniest joke. "I'd better get back to my table. Thank you for the wine, Dallas. I hope to be seeing more of you around town."

"Bye now," he said, then Addie's shoes walked off leaving only the pair of adorable heels standing by. All went silent.

I stayed there, scrunched on all fours.

"Would the lady under the table like a glass of wine, as well?" Emily asked, using a hushed tone.

I slid upward and into my shadowed chair, my humiliation complete. "Sorry, I . . . um . . ." There really was no decent excuse to be made. "Fill my wine glass to the rim, please."

Emily nodded, keeping a straight face as she poured me a full glass before taking our orders and then rushing off. Very professional. Although I'd bet money she was laughing with her co-workers in the kitchen right about now.

"Okay, let's hear it." Dallas took a swig of wine and then made a circling gesture with his hand. "Does this have anything to do with your parents? I get ducking Addie Wilcox, but your folks?"

"It's complicated." I reached out to the makeshift candlelight centerpiece, unscrewing the low-watt bulb to make our table even dimmer. Then I ducked down in my chair, sipped my wine, wishing I'd been straight with my parents from day one. The red wine tasted rich and velvety, clinging to my tongue and sending warmth spiraling through my body. The silence at our table was deafening. I lifted my lashes, meeting caramel-brown eyes that were peering at me with concern. I let out a breath. "My parents don't know I'm opening a beauty salon. In fact, they don't know I'm a licensed cosmetologist."

His eyes widened. He choked on his wine. I could see my mom and dad from here. Thankfully they were seated in a way that their heads were turned away from us, at least for the moment and I was pretty sure the distance and the dimness would keep me from being spotted.

"Why not? You should be proud of yourself."

Warmth flowed through me, either from his words or the wine, or both. "I didn't tell my parents how I spent my inheritance from my grandparents. They thought I was using the funds to get an MBA. Instead, I went to the beauty academy. Now I'm opening my own salon."

His eyes gleamed. "You've changed, Morgan. The girl I knew would've never stood up for herself like that. Kudos."

"Thanks." I smiled, feeling a sudden connection with him. We hadn't seen each other in eight years, but he did know me. We'd grown up together. It was wonderful feeling understood. "I feel bad keeping this secret from them. I'd planned to tell them last night, but then thought they might take the news better if the salon were fixed up first. If they catch me in this lie, I'll be guilty as charged."

"If I need help with a life of crime I'll call you," he joked, winking at me.

I guffawed. "Me? You were a total juvenile delinquent."

The arrival of our meals paused our conversation. I stared down at a glorious steak, still sizzling and crusted to perfection. I laid my napkin across my lap and then picked up my knife and fork.

Dallas's hands stilled on his utensils. "My criminal behavior is highly exaggerated."

"Is that so?" I chewed my steak slowly, remembering back. "Let me see. I remember you stealing the Christmas sled and taking it for a joyride one year . . ."

"Okay, guilty on that one." He cut a bite of his steak and nodded. "But they'd decided not to give out rides that year, remember? There were a bunch of foster kids living in the group home, who had been excited about going but then they announced the rides were off. So, I stole the sled. Yes, that was wrong. But my motives were good *and* I didn't rat out a single rider when I got caught, because those kids had it hard enough already. They didn't need a record to top of everything else."

"That was sweet of you." My heart melted. I'd always been told he'd stolen the sled out of sheer wildness. I'd had no idea that he'd taken the foster kids from the group home out for the rides they had been eagerly anticipating.

My heart went from melting to pounding as I saw Addie traipsing across the dining room, heading straight for my parents. The bite I tried to swallow felt stuck in my throat as Addie hugged my folks and began chatting with them, her hands waving wildly in the air.

I guzzled the rest of my wine. "Uh-oh."

"What is it?" he asked.

"Addie," I said, croaking the word out.

He glanced over his shoulder. "Want me to try to stop her?"

"You'd do that for me?" I asked, touched as I watched Addie walk off. I saw my mother's smile, which had been wide and warm, slowly die. She reached for her purse. My heart gave off a few loud and fast thumps. I fought to breathe normally. "Maybe it's okay. Maybe Addie didn't tell her about seeing me in town earlier."

My mother was digging for something and I hoped it was car keys. Instead, she took out a phone and tapped on the screen.

A loud ring came from my purse. I dived for it, my hands sliding inside to grab my phone and cut off the ringer. Oh, please, please let her not have heard my phone ringing across the restaurant. Luckily, she didn't look my way.

"Coast is clear." Dallas turned back to me, reaching for his wine.

My gaze locked with his as he took a sip. "I'm so sorry to

ruin your dinner, but I have to get out of here right now," I said, hoping he didn't get upset.

To my surprise, he agreed and went to get the check.

* * *

We left The Chop House minutes later and the further we drove out of town the further away my problems seemed, and the more the near run-in with my parents slipped from my mind. Distraction felt good right now. I was beyond curious to find out where Dallas lived.

He turned down a private road until a small house came into view, nestled on a high ridge, acres of pines and firs surrounding it. I imagined how beautiful the area would look when covered in a blanket of pure white, but it wasn't quite cold enough for much snow yet even at this elevation and time of year.

Dallas pulled into his driveway. The modest house was made of stone and wood, with tall windows lit up with golden light coming from inside. The porch looked like the perfect place to sit and take in this idyllic setting with its breathtaking mountain views.

I turned to Dallas. "Your place is beautiful. How long have you lived here?"

"Almost a year." He cut the engine and grabbed our "to go" bags from The Chop House, which Emily had quickly packed for us when she'd discovered we were high-tailing it out of there with only a minute's notice. I hoped he'd given her a big tip. "I loved this house from the moment I laid eyes on it," he said. "The place immediately felt like home, as crazy as that sounds."

"It's a special place, remote and peaceful. I can see why

you love it." I got out of the truck and headed up the short walkway beside him. "Are those mullioned windows?"

"Good eye," he said, his tone indicated his surprise that I'd named that type of window. "Someone was going to throw them out, so I bought them and installed them myself."

"They're amazing," I said, as he unlocked the front door. My gaze returned to the charming windows. The frames and decorative strips of metal and wood ran in long vertical and horizontal pieces, holding the small panes of glass into place. Beautiful.

"Mullioned windows are rarely made anymore since people generally prefer one large pane of glass with a simple frame." He opened the door, waiting for me to go inside first before he followed, shutting the door behind us. "I was lucky to find them."

"You found the windows in town?" I asked.

He shook his head. "I was in Idaho about six months ago, delivering furniture to a store that takes pieces on consignment. On my way out of town, I drove by this hundred-year-old Tudor home. The house was a teardown since it was too far gone to save. I love working with reclaimed stuff. When I saw they were about to demolish the house, I offered to buy the windows and they sold them to me."

"What a great history your windows have," I said, admiring his passion and how he went after his dreams. My awe grew as we walked through the hallway into a great room with wide, planked floors. I glanced down at the gleaming wood and then took in the cozy living room, the incredible windows, and the beautiful furniture. I ran my fingers over the back of a brown leather sofa by the fireplace. "I saw this sofa in a furniture store in Miami."

"Not possible," he said, setting the dinner bags on a rustic dining table that appeared made of reclaimed pine, complete with knots and imperfections. "I made that sofa myself."

My mouth dropped open. "For real?"

Pride lit up his face. "I made all the furniture here."

"Wow, that's impressive," I said, swiveling in a slow circle taking in the dining table with four chairs and a matching long bench, a low coffee table that featured carved legs, and a club chair upholstered in a geometric pattern that really popped against the rest of the rustic furniture. "Your work is amazing, Dallas."

"Thank you." His mouth curved upward and he winked at me before heading to the kitchen. He opened a drawer, reached inside, and then returned to the table with forks and knives.

I surveyed the living room and frowned, trying to figure out what was missing. Finally, I snapped my fingers. "No tree."

"Huh?" He stood beside the table, staring at me like I'd spoken a foreign language.

"You don't have a Christmas tree." I joined him at the table and he gestured for me to take a seat. "Your tree would look perfect next to those windows. Why don't you have a tree up yet?"

He filled our plates and then sat down, his expression impassive. "I don't get a tree."

"Since when?" I asked, diving into what was left of my steak as he filled glasses of red wine for us. "You were always crazy about Christmas. You and my brother both." A memory hit me then. "Don't you remember the time you two built a sleigh out of old go-karts?"

Dallas swallowed his bite, and then laughed. "I can't believe you remember that. Connor and I were about twelve, so you were only ten."

"How could I forget?" I leaned toward him, my fork in one

hand and my other hand resting on the table's silky wood surface. "You two forgot to take into consideration there would be snow and that the brakes were touchy. When you flew around that corner, you must've hit the brake hard because I watched you fly right out of that thing and sail into a snow bank," I said, laughing at the scene in my mind.

Dallas chuckled, taking a bite of steak. "Yeah, your brother landed right beside me as I recall. And you went running home to tell on us. Again."

We both laughed until my stomach hurt. Dallas sobered up first and wiped his eyes before finishing off his steak and potatoes. His gaze drifted to the windows and I wondered if he was picturing a tree there like I was. I also remembered he hadn't answered my question.

"So, why no tree?" I took my last bite of steak and then set my fork down. I reached for my wine glass and our eyes met, the comfortable energy between us suddenly turning tense.

"Too many bad memories." He lifted his wine glass. The large gulp he took told me how uncomfortable he was on this subject. I wondered what bad memories he was talking about but wasn't sure if I should pry.

I twisted my lips to one side. "I love this dining table. Is this the kind of furniture you'll be selling at the store?" I asked, vaguely remembering that my plan was to get him out of my business space, not give him encouragement to stay there.

He nodded. "I have stock built up that I keep in a back building on my property. Since we've both finished dinner, why don't we sit by the fireplace and I'll light a fire?"

The idea of sitting beside him on that sofa, in front of a fire, and with a glass of wine sounded so . . . incredibly romantic. My brain told me to say no, but I must've indulged in too much wine. Or maybe that close call at the restaurant had unhinged me. Either way, I bit my lip, unable to resist. "That sounds lovely. Let me help you clean up first."

We cleared the table and then took our glasses to the couch. I perched on the edge, watching him light the fire. Then he hit a dimmer switch and the room darkened in the corners but the fire burned a cheerful orange-red. I stared at those flames, mesmerized.

He sat next to me, the scent of his woodsy cologne making my belly flutter. The mood was intimate and romantic, with shadows on the walls cast by the flickering firelight. His thigh brushed mine, sending ripples of goosebumps up my arms.

The coziness of the room and the decadent plushness of the sofa lulled me for a moment, inviting fantasies of a long kiss and the feel of his arms around me. The pull of that fantasy was so strong that I actually leaned closer to him, my shoulder meeting his solid body with a brush that sent flitters of excitement tingling through me.

This was *not* a good thing.

I jerked back and turned away from him, my gaze landing on a silver-framed photograph sitting on the fireplace mantel. "Is that you as a boy?" I asked, recognizing a younger version of Dallas that must've been from his early high school days sitting next to an older gentleman with a plaid shirt. "Who's that with you? Your dad?"

He sucked in breath. "My uncle."

The pain in his voice was clear, which tugged at my heartstrings. "Are you two close?" I asked, assuming he'd say yes. After all, people didn't generally keep pictures on the mantel if they weren't of someone close to them.

"Uncle Richard and I are as close as we can be, I guess." He raked a hand through his hair and then popped off the couch. Even though he'd just set the fire up, he went to the fireplace, lifted the poker and jammed it into the logs, which burned merrily and showed no sign of abating any time soon. I stood, not sure why he looked so upset.

"Dallas?" I went to him, placing my hand on his arm, which felt rigid and stiff beneath my fingers. My gaze flew to the photo of the happy boy, making me wonder what was going on. "Are you okay? I didn't mean to hit a nerve."

"It's not your fault." He set the poker back in the rack, leaned against the wall, shoving his hands in his pockets. "I just don't usually talk about him."

I felt more confused than ever. Did that mean he never had people over who asked about the photo? Addie Wilcox had mentioned he'd been holed up in this house. Maybe she'd been right.

"You're obviously upset." I squeezed his arm and leaned against the wall so we were facing each other. "We can talk about it if you want . . ."

The fire outlined his rugged body, but left his face in the shadows. Even so, I could see that his forehead creased and the corners of his mouth turned downward.

"I'm still trying to live it all down," he said, his voice hoarse.

A chill vibrated through me. I moved closer to him. My pulse raced and something clicked in my memory. "Does this have to do with what happened in high school?"

He leveled me with his gaze. "It has everything to do with it."

My fingers twisted together. "I heard rumors, but I never knew the real story. There was an accident, right?"

His jaw tightened. "The accident was my fault. If that's what you heard."

"I'd rather hear the truth, directly from you." I lifted the frame from the mantel and stared down at the picture. "You two look happy together."

"You know my dad's an alcoholic, right?" He waited and finally nodded when I didn't answer. "He's known as the town drunk, so you've heard. Bad rumors even get back to me. But that one's true. My dad started drinking after my mom left us. He couldn't handle raising me alone. Uncle Richard stepped in, took me under his wing."

My throat tightened. "Your uncle sounds like a nice man."

"The best," he said, his jaw tightening. "One night during my senior year, my dad asked me to wake him in the morning for work at the sawmill. My uncle worked there, too. I'd even had part-time jobs there. But that weekend, I'd been out late partying and forgot to set the alarm."

"People forget things. It happens. Did he miss work that day?"

"Just the morning. But that was enough." His brown eyes turned stormy with emotion. "There's a rule at the sawmill that if you have to check the conveyor belt, you padlock the switch in the control room when you turn the machines off. That way everyone knows there's a person in the room. It's a safety thing. On the day my dad didn't show up for work, one of their co-workers—a guy named Brian—came in to find the machine off. There was no padlock, so he assumed nobody was in the room and he turned it on. My uncle was in the room."

A sinking feeling filled my gut. "What happened?"

His eyes closed for a moment and he breathed in slowly. "One of the logs jammed on the conveyor belt. The pressure built up until it spun off and hit Uncle Richard in the head. The accident left him severely brain damaged. He now lives in a care facility in town and barely recognizes who I am."

"I'm so sorry." My vision blurred. I reached for his hand, squeezing it. "What a terrible accident, but that's not your fault."

"My uncle probably didn't put the padlock on because he was rushing, doing the work of two men so my dad wouldn't get in trouble for being late to work."

My chest tightened. "You are *not* to blame for that."

"If I'd woken my dad up like I was supposed to then they both would've been at work. My uncle wouldn't have been hurrying and skipping safety precautions."

"You don't know what made him forget to put that padlock on, but that wasn't your responsibility." I put my hand on his shoulder and stared into his eyes, hoping he'd believe me. "He could've been distracted by something else on his mind. There are so many variables. Maybe the accident would have happened anyway."

His lips went flat. "Maybe not."

My heart ached for him. "You were just a kid and shouldn't be responsible for waking a grown man up in the morning."

"Uncle Richard had acted like a buffer between my dad and me. After the accident, my dad's drinking got worse. He got worse. The accident happened just before Christmas. I'd decorated a Christmas tree for us that year as a gift to my dad. He picked it up and threw it at me."

I gasped. My hand flew to my mouth. I'd been so worried about my relationship with my parents and Dallas had been through so much worse than I could ever imagine. I looked away, letting my hair fall against my cheek to hide the horror that was surely visible all over my face.

"After graduation, I joined the Marines. I served four years, then got a job in Idaho and didn't speak to my dad for seven years." His fingers slid through my hair, tucking my hair behind my ear, and playing with the ends until I looked up at him. "When my aunt passed away last year, I decided it was time to come home. Somebody needed to be here for my uncle."

I swallowed the lump in my throat. "Have you seen your dad?"

"We saw each other at the funeral. He acknowledged me, but it wasn't exactly a happy family reunion. He's retired from the sawmill and doesn't have much to live on. I drop by once every couple of weeks to make sure his refrigerator is stocked. That's the extent of our relationship."

"I'm sorry." I shook my head, knowing those two words weren't close to conveying how much my heart broke for him. How much I admired his loyalty to his uncle and even to his dad, especially after how he'd been raised. "I didn't know that's why you returned home."

"Why did you come back here, Morgan?" His fingers trailed along my jawline, the backs of them brushing my cheek. "You're running a big risk with your folks—especially since you can't hide forever. You could have set up your own salon in Miami. So what brought you home?"

Home. The word settled under my ribs, went straight into my heart.

I stared into his eyes. "I missed Christmas Mountain."

It was the simplest truth, and the only one I could think of to give.

"I missed *you*," he whispered. Then his expression softened and he cupped my face in his hands, slanting his head as he moved closer. I held my breath and he leaned forward until our mouths were close, only a whisper apart.

Under his spell, I rose onto my toes and pressed my lips to his. His mouth was warm. The kiss was soft and sweet, holding all of the emotion of what he'd just shared with me. Then his mouth opened and his tongue connected with mine, tasting warm and velvety like the wine we'd both had. Butterflies danced in my belly and I felt like I was floating.

For most of my youth, I'd dreamed of kissing Dallas, and

now all of those feelings washed over me, blanketing me in a sea of warmth that told me I hadn't been brought home to Christmas Mountain only for my mentor, or for my career, or for my family, but for him.

The fireplace crackled as we kissed again and again. My whole body lit up with this strong electrical current passing back and forth between us, increasing as the kisses lengthened and deepened. Oh, my.

Somewhere in the back of my mind I knew there was no chance of implementing the plot to get him out of my business space via over-feminizing the salon. Whatever. I preferred more neutral tones anyway.

Suddenly he pulled back, studying me through heavy-lidded eyes. I let out a heavenly sigh and smiled at him. His lips curved upward and the sadness in his eyes was gone. His arms slipped around me and pulled me close, making me melt against him.

My toes literally curled inside my shoes as he continued kissing me senseless.

CHAPTER FIVE

The next morning, I was enjoying a bowl of cereal and coffee when I heard the front door of the townhome close. A moment later Ruby entered the kitchen with a large bag in one hand and a smile on her face. I wished I looked as happy as she did this morning.

I'd stayed at Dallas's house way too late. Eventually we'd moved to the couch and talked until the fire went out. I had to admit there was also more kissing. Swoon. But when I got home, I listened to a voicemail from my mom and reality hit me hard. I'd been home for two days and still hadn't told them about my new career. Or that my new business shared spaced with the man my mom blamed for my sister's death. On top of that, I seemed to have fallen for him.

But what was I supposed say? "Surprise! I'm going to style hair instead of working at your bank. I'll give a great discount, though. And Dallas Parker? He'll be working with me and kissing me on the side. Merry Christmas!"

Yeah, that would not fly well.

"Hello? Earth to Morgan, come in please..."

"Huh?" I looked over at Ruby, realizing I'd slumped my

chin on my fist and spilled a spoonful of honey oats in my lap. "Oh, no!"

She threw a kitchen towel at me. I mopped up the oats, but they left a not-so-sexy wet splotch on my knee. Lovely.

"Guess someone needs a second cup of coffee." She laughed.

"Sorry." I hung my head in shame, wondering what she'd been saying to me. Then I got distracted by her bag. "What on earth were you shopping for so early this morning?" I asked.

The bag crinkled as she reached inside it. Her smile turned impish. "It's not *that* early. You slept in pretty late, probably because you were out late. Or at least I think you were since I didn't hear you come home before I went to bed."

"No comment." I gulped the coffee, stalling for time to think of an answer to where I'd been. Ruby gave me a suspicious look before pulling plain Christmas tree bulbs from the bag and lining them up on the table. I set the cup down. "Are you painting Christmas ornaments?"

She nodded and fished around in the bag some more. "I'm hoping you'll help. You can paint an angel like nobody's business."

"Angels have always been my favorite," I said, my mood momentarily lifting.

She set a tray of paints and a pack of brushes on the table and went to the coffee pot. She poured herself a cup and came back. "So . . . ?"

"Yes, I'll paint an angel," I said, knowing that wasn't what she really wanted to know. I couldn't help envying how perky she looked this morning. She wore a pretty red sweater, a black wool skirt with black tights underneath, low-heeled ankle boots, and a pair of earrings shaped like dangling Santas. Her blonde hair was pinned up in a bun, showing off those festive earrings.

I glanced down at my flannel pajama pants, an old long-sleeved shirt, and a set of fuzzy slippers. Ugh. I so needed to get more in the Christmas spirit. I took my bowl to the sink, rinsed it, and put it into the dishwasher. Then I poured more coffee and headed back to the table.

"Paint as many as you can." Ruby pushed a few silver and red balls toward me, and a set of paints and brushes. "The Christmas Tree Lighting Ceremony is tonight. I got roped into helping with the ornaments."

I took a brush from the container. "The Christmas Tree Lighting Ceremony is such a wonderful tradition."

Ruby dipped a brush into paint and nodded. "I'm so behind, though. Work has been insane since they announced that this year they want to do a doggie parade down Main Street."

My eyebrows went up. "Come again?"

Ruby laughed. "Not even kidding. I've been swamped by people who are desperate to get their dogs trained to stop eating the antlers, ears, and other things on the costumes their dogs will be wearing in the parade. Not to mention they want to ensure their pooches behave while walking with a crowd of spectators cheering."

"Sounds super festive." I started painting an angel with a blue dress.

"Addie Wilcox is having sheer fits because she's so sure Bertie Grier's Great Danes are going to eclipse Addie's little Pomeranian in the parade."

"Huh," I mumbled, because that information was too much for my under-caffeinated brain. I dipped a brush into the paint and gave the angel dark hair. "Well, that would be a tragedy."

Ruby said, "I'm sure. I don't even know if Addie's Pom

knows how to walk. Every time I see the poor dog she's toting him. But you still haven't answered my question."

I added glowing wings to the angel. "What question?"

"So . . . what were you up to last night?" Her tone was playful and a smile spread across her face. "You couldn't have been at the beauty salon that late."

Time to come clean. "I went to dinner with Dallas."

"You did?" Ruby dropped the bulb she'd been holding, which rolled off the table and onto the floor. I winced at the sound of glass shattering. Ruby jumped to her feet and pulled a broom from the closet. "Tell me everything. Did you try the prime rib special? Was it awesome?"

"It was awful."

Ruby began sweeping up the pieces. "Why?"

"My folks were at the restaurant and so was Addie Wilcox, who saw me outside my new business space yesterday." I groaned, remembering how hard my heart had pounded. It was a wonder I didn't need a cardiologist after that episode. "Addie would've outed me to my parents and she nearly spotted me. I had to hide under the table."

"You didn't!"

"I did," I said, remembering what a good sport Dallas had been about the whole thing. "I think Addie might have told my mom where she saw me. She went over to Mom and Dad's table and said something to them. A minute later my mom called me. I silenced the phone and then Dallas had to smuggle me and our dinners out of the restaurant."

Ruby finished disposing of the broken bulb and took a seat. "You should call your mom and tell her everything. She's going to find out sooner or later and the longer you wait—"

"I know." I glanced out the kitchen window. Trees and houses were decorated with colorful twinkling lights, looking like something out of a fairytale. "I will tell them, I just want to get the place fixed up a little first. They'll take it better that way. Plus, my mom's not going to be thrilled I'm sharing the space with Dallas." I sighed, thinking of the impending blow-up. "Do you remember the rumors about Dallas in high school?"

"Sure." Ruby blotted her paintbrush and then looked at me. "Just that he was trouble. But he was always nice to me. Remember the fun we had together as kids?"

"Yeah, I remember."

The tip of Ruby's paintbrush jabbed into the air in my direction. "Remember how he almost killed your brother with that go-kart stunt."

"To be fair, Connor was just as guilty. He did make his own go-kart sleigh."

"True." Ruby's eyebrows rose upward. "But Dallas did earn his bad boy rep fair and square. There was that time he stole the frogs from the biology lab and lined them up in the cafeteria under a big old sign that read *murder victims*."

I sipped coffee and began to work on a second angel. "To be fair, nobody should have to dissect a frog. It's just gross. And not fair to the frogs. Besides, I didn't hear you complaining when the school decided we couldn't use them and waived that year's dissection test."

"You sure like to defend Dallas Parker." Ruby smiled knowingly. "But how can you defend him when he took Coach Borden's golf cart for a joyride. He's also the one that dared the track team guys to jump from the water tower."

"None of them did, though," I pointed out. "*He* did. Broke his leg as I recall."

"Which goes to show that even if he can't talk someone else into doing something crazy he's totally committed to doing it himself."

I couldn't even argue with that one. I gave the angel a set of rosy cheeks and then my gaze flicked to hers. "What have you heard about the accident involving his uncle?"

"Let me think." Ruby finished her bulb and set it on a paper towel to dry. "There were various stories floating around about the details. Mostly, I heard his dad said the accident was Dallas's fault. I mean, why would his dad say that if it wasn't?"

"Because his dad is a mean drunk!" I snapped and then cringed. I gave her an apologetic look, but I thought it was terrible the way he'd neglected Dallas and then blamed him for the accident. My heart hurt for him. He already blamed himself, which was bad enough. But to have the whole town believe he was to blame for that tragedy? No wonder he'd left town after graduation. "The accident wasn't his fault. He wasn't even there that day."

"Wasn't where?" she asked.

"At the sawmill the day of the accident. Dallas worked there part-time, but that was one of his days off. He wasn't anywhere around there when it happened." I got up and went to the counter, staring out the window again. The sun twinkled off the trees, sending a glow of light around each branch. "Why do people believe rumors so easily?"

"Wait a minute." Ruby made a clucking sound with her tongue. "You sound super protective of Dallas. I thought you wanted him out of your salon."

"I did want him out of my salon." I turned around, imagining all of the crazy scenarios in keeping our businesses together in the same space. "I mean, come on, opening a furniture store slash beauty salon? Just what every small town needs. No way is that going to work. What would our slogan be, come for the perms and stay for the sofas?"

Ruby wiped her fingers on a paper towel. "That's actually kind of catchy."

I groaned. "No. It isn't. It's—

Ding-dong. Ding-dong. Ruby's doorbell cut me off. I glanced down at my pajamas and gave her a sheepish, pleading smile. "Well, it's obviously not for me."

She took the hint and stood. "Probably someone selling something. I'll get it."

"Thanks." I took a deep breath as she walked out of the room.

Why was everyone so quick to blame Dallas for his uncle's accident? I could make a long list of reasons why it wasn't his fault. My childhood crush had turned into much more after last night. I was thinking hard about my complicated feelings for Dallas that at first I didn't even register the familiar voice talking to Ruby.

Then it hit me.

I startled out of my thoughts and looked up to see my brother, Connor, walking toward me. He had the same pear-green eyes as I did, his dark hair was neatly combed back, and he had on what looked like a very expensive half-zip sweater. He also wore a knowing smirk.

"Hey, sis. Mom just called me. You're in so much trouble."

And with those words, my heart took to pounding against my ribs again.

I looked down at the bulbs of angels staring up at me with their big blue eyes and pink mouths. It was as if they were trying to tell me I'd run out of time and the whole mess I'd created with my secrets—too many to count at this point—was about to blow up in my face.

CHAPTER SIX

I jumped up from the table and dashed toward Connor, throwing my arms around my big brother. "Hey, you. We haven't seen each other since you came down to Miami last year for our family cruise."

Connor hugged me back. "You're glad to see me even if I am the bearer of bad news?"

"I'm not exactly excited about *that* part." I released him and stepped back.

He gave me a quick once-over. "Whoa, look at you. Not sure I even want the full story of what's going on."

I looked down at my pajamas, imagining the dark circles that had to be under my eyes. "No, you probably don't want to know." Connor made a big show of looking at his watch and coughing into his hand. I rolled my eyes. "I know. I overslept. Sue me."

Connor rubbed his neck with one hand, a sure sign he was nervous about something. "Listen, odds are Mom knows you're here. At Ruby's, I mean. You haven't answered her texts this morning and by now she's called or dropped by to visit every old friend you have here. It's probably a good idea to get out of here for a while. You want to take a ride?"

"Let me get dressed." I raced to my room and grabbed clothes, yanking on a blue long-sleeve top, a pair of jeans, my coat and boots. I came back out after pulling my hair up in a messy twist, knowing I should probably put on makeup in case we did run into Mom so she'd think I had my life totally together (yeah, right). But I was more worried about getting out of the townhome before she could show up and corner me than I was about running into her in town.

Connor wasn't wrong about our mom. Ivy Reed was unstoppable once she decided to do something and what she'd apparently decided to do right then was locate her wayward daughter. I had no doubt she'd already done just as he said. The only thing that had saved me so far was that Ruby's house was the furthest from Mom's so it would be the last one she tried.

We said bye to Ruby and went out the front door. "Let's take my SUV," I said.

"Not a chance." Connor shook his head. "If Mom finds my car here then she'll know I helped you escape her clutches. Or she'll think Ruby and I are dating and then it's all over for me. She'll tell me Ruby is the best match I could ever hope to make and then she'll start dropping not-so-subtle hints about how much she wants grandchildren and a big wedding to throw. Believe me. She's been relentless."

I couldn't help laughing as we ambled down the walkway. My mom did seem to be on his case lately about settling down.

"Glad you find my misery amusing." He shot a glance at me. "I don't mind saving your bacon, sis, but no way do I want her trying to marry me off. And you know she would if she thinks I'm dating someone special, which is not the case.

Since your SUV is safe in Ruby's garage, your location will still be a mystery for a little while longer."

I huffed out a breath. "Until she decides to break into Ruby's garage . . ."

Connor pressed a button on his key fob, unlocking the expensive sedan parked at the curb. "You brought this on yourself, sis."

"I hope she marries you off by spring," I retorted, opening the passenger's side and slipping into the leather seat. "Wow. This is *plush*. When did you get a new car?"

He started the engine and grinned. "Work bonus."

"Must be nice being the star child." I batted my eyes at him as we pulled away from the townhome. "You still managing the loan department at good ole Reed Bank?"

"Yes." He squirmed, tossing me an annoyed look. "Just because you didn't want to go into the family business doesn't mean I have to rebel. I wanted to work at the bank. I actually like working for Dad."

"My life would be so much simpler if I'd wanted that, too." I stared out the window as we headed down the winding road that led toward downtown.

In most of the neighborhoods, people were outside decorating for Christmas. My spirits floated upward at the sight. I knew that the air outside was cold and crisp enough to bring a rosy flush to a cheek. I considered rolling down the windows to feel that air flowing over my face, but I also liked the feeling of being warm and cozy inside.

I turned away from the scenery. "So things are going well at the bank?"

"Yep." He kept a hand on the wheel and glanced over at me. "Tourism has been down lately in Christmas Mountain. The *Herald* posts a new article about it every week. So, many businesses are applying for loans to make it through. How're things in the renegade beautician business?"

I had to laugh at his apt description. "Not great, actually." I chewed my bottom lip. "Lots of challenges going on in that department. Are you and Dallas Parker still close?"

"Dallas?" Connor turned the wheel, driving past a Christmas tree lot. "We lost touch after he went into the military. I haven't seen him since he's been back. I've been working a lot."

"That's too bad." I paused, chewing on my thumbnail. "I can't believe Dallas's own dad told everyone that he was to blame for that accident with his uncle."

Connor shot me a look. "You do know his dad drinks, right? Not exactly making stellar decisions."

"Yeah, but still. A parent is supposed to be there to protect you. Not sell you out."

"That was pretty brutal." Connor pulled into the empty parking lot that sat next to the Falls. "He wasn't always such a crummy dad. Dallas's mom took off when he was around eight years old and that's when his dad started drinking. Went downhill from there."

"I don't remember any of that."

"You were younger than us." Connor grabbed the keys and opened his door. "Anyway, Dallas used to hope he and his dad would get back to where they were before she left, but it never happened. Dallas's uncle stepped in as a father figure until the accident."

I pulled on the door handle and stepped out onto the sidewalk. "How awful."

"Yeah, his uncle was the only good role model in his life. Dallas took his uncle's accident hard and being blamed for it devastated him. He's the kind of guy who goes silent when he's hurting. That's probably why he left town. I should have tried harder to reach him."

"We all should've tried harder to be there for him," I said, thinking of how I'd avoided Dallas after Grace's death. I'd felt guilty hanging around him knowing my mom blamed him for Grace's terrible fall. There were times when my mom hadn't been around and then I'd hang with Dallas and Connor, but not like when we still had Grace.

We hiked up the steps leading to the spot beside the waterfall. The Falls were pouring down with a soothing sound, splashing against the gray and black rocks into the natural pool at the bottom. Stands of pine trees covered the sides of the mountain, framing the Falls. Happiness hit again. Miami was amazing and wonderful but there was no feeling like being home.

We walked past The Sharing Tree and Kissing Bench, which reminded me of that day with Tom when Dallas had gotten in his face. They'd argued and pushed each other, before Dallas finally socked him in the jaw. I remembered my astonishment and confusion. After the incident, my mom reminded me that Dallas had always been bad news, reckless and unsafe. I never really saw him that way, but sometimes I'd wonder if she was right.

"Why the interest in Dallas?" Connor nudged me with his elbow. "Don't tell me you still have a crush on him."

"I never had a crush on him," I lied.

"You can't fool me, sis. I clearly remember you stalking him when we were kids."

I let out an indignant yelp. "I didn't *stalk* him."

I may have followed him from a respectable distance....

"Sure you did." Connor leaned against the railing by the Falls, gripping the metal bar with his gloved fingers. "You'd practically wait by the door when you knew he was coming over and then you'd follow us on our adventures. You were always hanging around."

"Your memory is whack," I said, and then huffed. My breath created long frosty plumes on the air that drifted up and away. "I was watching out for you two trouble makers. Good thing, since you were always doing stuff that could get you hurt. Like that go-kart stunt."

His eyes danced. "Don't ever tell Mom, but as scary as that day was . . . it was still the most fun I ever had in my life. Lots of good memories with Dallas."

"You two used to be best friends." I glanced over at my brother, who looked deep in thought. "It's Christmastime. What better reason to renew friendships?"

"Maybe you're right." He tilted his head thoughtfully. "Have you seen Dallas since you arrived? You must've since you're bringing him up."

I groaned a little. "When I arrived in town, I went to the business space I rented for my salon and found him there. Turns out he has a lease for the place, too."

Connor's mouth twitched. "Say what?"

"He's opening a furniture store." I turned to stare down at the crashing waters below. "How am I supposed to promote a professional beauty salon with half the space as a furniture store?"

"Maybe you could work out a deal to sell chairs instead of conditioner while clients get their hair done? I'd bet there's a higher profit on a chair over a bottle of shampoo, or whatever."

"That's not helpful, thanks."

He shrugged. "What are you going to do then?"

"I don't know." I admitted bleakly. "He's actually been really helpful to have around. Yesterday, I managed to blow a fuse or whatever. All the electricity went out. Dallas called and hired an electrician to take care of the problem, which might be fixed already. I should probably be at the salon right now. The sooner I fix it up, the sooner I can try to get mom and dad excited about my new venture, the C.M. Salon."

"Aren't initials a bit pretentious, sis?" he asked, flicking some drops of water on the railing at my face.

I flicked a good amount back at him.

Connor hollered, "Cold. That's cold!"

I jutted out my chin. "So is calling my business name pretentious."

"C.M. Salon . . ." He chuckled. "Do the initials stand for curl and mold? Cut and make over? Clip and magnificent?"

"Christmas Mountain, you dweeb . . ." I searched for a puddle to flick more water at him.

He held his hands up. "Truce?"

"For now. And only because I need to get to the salon and start working on it before Dallas decorates the whole place like the showroom of a furniture store."

"Dallas is a good guy. He wouldn't do that," he said, taking the lead as we headed back to the stairs. Then Connor paused, taking hold of my arm. "Seriously, Morgan. Why are you so against telling Mom and Dad about your new career?"

I guffawed and then held up a hand to tick off the reasons on my fingers. "One, they're going to be upset that I was secretive about how I spent my trust. They'd pushed me to get an MBA, remember? Two, they'll be disappointed I gave up a business career to open a beauty salon. Three, there's no way they will see being a beautician as something impressive, even though I love it. Basically, I'll feel like I've disappointed them and . . . I don't want them to talk me out of my dream."

"They're going to be more upset the longer you wait. But it's your trust to spend the way you want. It's not like Grandma and Grandpa put any conditions on it. So, tell them. You don't know for sure that they'll be disappointed until you try."

All my happiness went flat and stale.

"Mom was controlling with both of us. But she's always put extra pressure on me." I looked away from him, my throat tightening. "I-I always knew I was the second daughter. You're the first and only son but I was the second daughter. I've had to live up to that and all the things Grace never got to do."

Connor's face twisted. "You're putting that on your shoulders? I get that we grew up with her ghost. It's sad that we lost her. It's terrible. But as much as we loved her, you should never feel like you need to take her place."

I let his words flow through my mind over and over. He made sense. But he didn't know the whole truth about Grace's accident. There was another secret I'd kept to myself and it haunted me. I glanced over at my big brother, who looked back at me so protectively. A big burden hung in my chest. Maybe if I told him, he'd understand why I felt so torn. I opened my mouth—

Ding-ding-ding! Ding-ding-ding! My cell phone went off in a familiar tune.

"I know that ringtone," Connor said.

"Yep." I sighed. My mom was calling me. No more texts. No more excuses. I knew it was time to face her. But now more than ever I worried how very disappointed she'd be in me.

CHAPTER SEVEN

The next day, I arrived at the salon slash furniture store and Dallas handed me two lattes from Sleigh Café and said we were going for a drive. So grateful for the coffee after a night of barely any sleep due to stressing over my problems, I agreed with no fuss.

We'd gotten a lot of work done yesterday with the electricity on again, but not enough that I felt comfortable showing my mom. Like a coward, I sent her a text that I wasn't feeling well—which was *so* the truth—and that when I was feeling better I had some news I wanted to share with her. A baby step in the right direction at least.

We drove up high in the mountains. Snow coated the ground and the wind hit Dallas's truck, making it rock slightly as we climbed higher. I had no idea where he was taking me. And I didn't care. I was just enjoying the ride, the view, and the coffee.

I stared out at the pine and fir trees, stripped of their leaves now, and the occasional glimpse of rock through the powdery dusting of snow. The air was cold and clear up there, so I could see for miles in all directions. My heart warmed. Home was where the heart was and right then I was exactly where I wanted to be.

The last few days had been a strain, despite my having run into my bracelet bff, Ashley Brooks, yesterday—she'd caught me crying on a bench by the Falls after Connor left—and how good it was to see her. I still had to face my mom eventually.

And, yeah, it had been awesome running into Lexi Townsend during the big Christmas Mountain tree lighting ceremony last night, and being with her and Ash made it so extra good to be home, but it's not like I could tell them about Dallas and those kisses when I still didn't know what to make of it. Dallas and I hadn't talked about it either.

Dallas shifted the truck into a lower gear and the engine caught and sent us up even higher before we landed on a hair-raising road that ran in a slim band along the side of the mountain. My fingernails became in real danger of shattering as I clutched at my seat.

"Where are we going?" I asked, finally.

"You said a tree would look nice next to my window at home." He glanced my way and we exchanged a look that warmed my belly. "We also need a tree for our front window at the store."

"I figured we'd go to Tinsel Tree Farm to get one, not the North Pole," I joked, and then glanced back at him. His jeans had patches of the glue he was using to put down the first part of the hardwood floors we had agreed upon for the space. His hair was messed up in a sexy way. He smelled of sawdust and lumber, a scent I was getting used to fast. Yum.

My heart gave a slight twist. He hadn't kissed me again since Saturday night, but then again I hadn't attempted to kiss him either. The last thing I needed to do was get mushy and weak in the knees around him when I didn't know what our kisses meant. To avoid confusing emotions, I'd focused on cleaning the salon and made lots of progress.

"A tree lot is not how I do things," he said.

"I can see that," I said, as we came to a halt in a small clearing that featured a gentle hill in the middle of a ring of trees. He cut the truck off and dusted more of the glue off his sleeve, or tried to. It seemed to be stuck pretty fast. More worry hit me. We had agreed on the floors, but how would I pay Dallas back if Coraline gave the salon to me?

"You ready?" He opened his door and I followed suit. The cold air slapped against my face, stinging my cheeks and sending a tingle to my blood. I yanked my gloves out of my coat pocket and put them on. He reached into the big metal toolbox in the back of the truck and pulled out a chainsaw. "Now, we find a tree."

"The perfect tree," I replied, wanting the perfect tree in the window under the C.M. Salon and Parker's Furniture "coming soon" sign we'd put up yesterday. We set off toward the wooded section on the other side of the clearing. The weather was a lot colder at this high elevation. My toes were cold even through the boots and the heavy socks I wore. I tilted my head back and looked up at the towering treetops. "We need a tree that's small enough to fit through the door and not hit the ceiling."

Dallas gestured to my right. "How about that one?"

I looked at the scrubby tree he'd pointed at, which was about two feet high. "Um, no." I laughed. "That's way too Charlie Brown."

He chuckled as we trudged on. My feet crunched across a patch of ice and then I slipped. Like lightning, he caught me and steadied me.

"Be careful," he said.

"I'll try," I said. But his hands on my arms had caused little shocks to bolt up along my central nervous system, making me so want to slip again.

We hiked along in amicable silence. The wind picked up, bringing the scent of pine. I shivered as we moved through the tree line and into the actual woods beyond the clearing.

"I saw Connor yesterday," I blurted.

"Yeah?" He stopped at a tree and knocked on the trunk, shook his head, and moved on. I had no idea what that meant, but I figured he knew better than I did. "How's Connor doing?"

"He's good." I stopped at a tree. I gave it a good rap, which didn't give me any better idea of whether or not the tree was right for us. It basically just made my knuckles sting. I winced. "We talked about you."

Dallas's gaze shot to mine. "What did you say?"

"Not much," I said, reassuring him I hadn't repeated anything personal he'd told me. Then I looked up at the top of the tree, which was about six feet tall with a wide and full set of branches. It was the best Christmas tree I'd ever seen. "This might be the one."

"I like it, too." He knelt down to study the trunk of the tree, lifting a few branches out of the way. He started fiddling with the button and blade on the chainsaw. "Good choice."

As I watched Dallas checking out the base of the tree, I squinted down at him. "Do you know what Connor said about me? He said I used to have a crush on you."

He looked up at me, a startled look on his face. "He thinks so, too, huh?"

I giggled, my belly fluttering. "He claimed that I stalked you."

Dallas blinked. Then the corners of his mouth tipped up. "You were always hanging around."

I batted his arm. "Maybe I was making sure neither of you got hurt."

He stood, leaving the chainsaw on the ground. Snow fell off his jeans and his grin grew wider as he came closer. "You had a lot of friends, Morgan. I might believe you were worried about Connor's safety. But there was no reason for you to worry about mine. Connor's right. You were definitely stalking me."

I bit my lip, lifting my lashes. "Maybe I did have a crush on you."

He reached for my hands. "Maybe?"

I shrugged. "I will confirm nothing."

"Say it." He suddenly tickled me and I erupted in a fit of laughter. I reached around him and pulled him down. We fell into a high drift of snow. I hollered as a chunk of snow slid into the neck of my coat and another chunk went up one sleeve. He continued tickling up and down my ribs, saying, "Admit you had a crush on me."

"I can't remember!" I laughed so hard, loving the feel of his body against mine. I rolled over, pinning him down, my hands bracing his on either side of his head. Then my breath left my lungs. "Okay, I did have a crush on you. Kind of a big one."

Creases formed on either side of his eyes and the corner of his mouth turned up. Then he lifted his head and I lowered mine at the same time. We kissed once before I pulled away. My heart pounded against my chest as I stared down at him, releasing his hands.

"Did you have a crush on me, Dallas? Is that why you punched my boyfriend at the Falls?"

His eyes locked with mine. "You deserved better than him."

"You didn't answer my other question."

He brushed my cheek with his fingers. "Yes, I had a crush on you."

Joy flitted around my heart. "Why didn't you ever say so?"

"I wasn't good enough for you, either."

I rested my hands against his shoulders. "I don't know why you'd think that..."

"Come on," he shifted, so he was propped up on one elbow and I was next to him. He smoothed my hair back behind my ear. "You deserved way better than me. I was a troublemaker and you were a good girl."

"I'm not such a good girl for sneaking around behind my parents' back with my career change," I said. And with you, I almost added.

"You're still a Reed."

"I'm the black sheep beautician."

His eyes twinkled. "How could I forget that? I mean, you're in my shop after all."

"Your shop?" Ugh. I opened my mouth to give a retort, but before I could his mouth came down on mine. Then I forgot about the cold snow beneath me, about the fact that I needed him out of *my* salon, and even the Christmas tree we came to find.

At that moment there was just us.

I kissed him with everything in me as his mouth claimed mine. Shivers skittered up and down my spine. My belly did a cartwheel. I opened my mouth and our tongues melted together. I could feel his warmth through every pore in my body. There was no way I could resist this man anymore. I didn't even want to. Wrapped in his arms and surrounded by the natural beauty all around me, I felt a peace I'd never known. This was the most flawless moment of my life and I never wanted it to end.

CHAPTER EIGHT

After working all week on the remodel for my salon, I made a point of visiting Ms. King on Friday. I pulled into her driveway and cut the engine off. The tip of the tree I'd brought for her waved downward over the windshield as if saying, "Hello!"

I hopped out of the SUV, surveying the small tree strapped to my roof that I'd picked up at Tinsel Tree Farm. I unhooked the cords that were securing the tree to the sports rack and then hauled the tree down to the ground. It stood as high as my chest and had full branches. Not too big and not too small. I dragged the tree up the driveway, noticing one of the lace curtains at the front window pull aside. I admired the front door, which was painted a peacock blue that contrasted sharply with the white house, and the door opened an instant later.

Ms. King stepped out. "Hello, Morgan. What a magnificent tree!"

"Hello, Ms. King." I waved enthusiastically at my choir teacher. This woman could always put a smile on my face. "I'm glad you like it."

I hauled the tree to her porch and propped it against the

house before looking at my beloved mentor. She wore a flowing white top that was cinched around her narrow waist by a wide belt, and slacks in a startling shade of purple. Her silver hair was brushed back, showing off opal earrings, not her birthstone but her favorite stone despite their reputation for being unlucky to those who weren't born with them as a birthstone. She pooh-poohed such claims.

She gave me a fast hug and then said, "It's so good to see you."

My reply stuck in my throat as I hugged her back, fighting to get a grip on the emotion that came toppling over me at the feel of her gaunt frame. Eight years ago, she'd been much larger. Now she was so thin I could feel the jutting out wings of her shoulder blades and collarbone.

Her swollen hands squeezed mine. "What made you bring me a tree?"

It had broken my heart when I'd heard she had no Christmas tree. She had no kids besides those of us she'd mentored, most of whom thought of her as a second mom. But I wasn't about to go down that road because I was here to cheer her up, not bring her down.

So I stepped back and put my hands on my hips. "The tree looked lonely and called to me. Since it didn't seem to be an ordinary tree, I figured it needed an extraordinary home."

Ms. King burst into laughter. Her eyes sparkled. "Well, then. Let's get the tree into the house and see what we can do to make it happy."

"Good plan." I smiled and brought the tree inside. Her house was a wonderland, filled with shelves crowded with books and trinkets from her travels as well as her collection of fine china—none of it matching but all of it lovingly used. Sometimes she'd set the china during her legendary dinner parties. My gaze lingered on a pink-and-gold cup that sat on a high shelf, exactly where I'd placed it so many years ago.

We'd known Melody King since we were young, since she helped put on the town Christmas extravaganza every year. Grace had always loved that cup and Ms. King had always let her use it. After Grace had died, I'd put it up high, saying I didn't want anyone else to use it. Ms. King had patted my shoulder, going along with it. The cup still sat on the high shelf with its delicate gold handle gleaming and the pink flowers around the rim.

I looked away from that cup and the memories that came along with it. Grace was the last thing I wanted to think about right now. It had been hard enough coming home. I didn't need to relive painful memories.

Ms. King clasped her hands together. "My Christmas decorations are in the spare bedroom. Let me get them."

She went around the corner and my gaze wandered around the rooms again. The front was an old-fashioned and traditional set up, with the rooms separated from the other. The bay windows at the front of the living room were huge and covered with curtains. Her furniture had come from all over and it showed. There were English sideboards and French chairs, antique and highly delicate, as well as beautifully paneled screens from China and Japan.

"I found the bulbs," Ms. King said, as she came back with a tree stand and a wooden box. She set the box on the table, while I got the tree in the holder and closed the vise down on the trunk to make sure the tree stayed in place.

"There! This works perfectly." I forced a smile, but couldn't help noticing her color wasn't good and her silver hair appeared dryer than usual.

She smiled, opening the wooden box. "Hmm. . . I have

another box of decorations, too. Before I fetch that, how about some coffee and a BLFGT sandwich?"

"I'd love that." I grinned, knowing Ms. King's penchant for serving Southern food. I loved how the South has a way of taking any food and making it Southern. A classic BLT was wonderful. But take off the ripe sliced tomato and put in a few slices of fried green tomato? Then you have a slice of fried heaven. "May I help make them?"

She dusted her hands together. "Why don't you slice and toast the bread, and cook the bacon, while I get the tomatoes ready?"

"Deal." I followed her into the kitchen, smiling when I saw it hadn't changed at all. The same chintz curtains hung at the kitchen window, the old table still stood by one wall and the chairs still wore the same cushions, chintz that matched the curtains. "Where do you keep the bread?"

Ms. King gestured to the pantry and I found a loaf of thick and soft French bread there. I came out of the pantry and she pointed to a cabinet. "The pan for bacon is in there."

I opened the cabinet and pulled out the pan. Then took the pack of bacon she had laid out on the counter and opened it, laying the strips out carefully before putting the bacon and the bread in the oven.

Ms. King battered the tomato slices and dropped them into a few inches of hot oil. I poured us both cups of coffee and then handed one to her. "Tell me what's going on in your world, Morgan."

I sipped the coffee and then cleared my throat. "Well, I came home. That's certainly new."

She laughed. "I see. Or at least I hope I see. Otherwise you're a figment of my very active imagination. That can't be good."

I had to laugh despite the grimness of the situation. "I'm

really here but it's been a bit surreal. I'm sort of hiding from my folks while I get the salon ready, hoping they'll approve of my career choice once they see how professional the salon looks. It's been a lot of work."

Ms. King flipped the frying green tomatoes. "Are you going to tell your parents about your change in careers soon?"

I wrinkled my nose. "Define 'soon.'"

Ms. King set the spatula aside and sipped her coffee. "You do know you can't hide from them forever?"

"I'm not trying to hide forever, just long enough to get the salon fixed in a way they might approve of." I bent to peer into the oven to see the bacon bubbling nicely and the bread toasting. "I've gotten a lot of work done this week."

Ms. King checked on the skillet. "How long until you open?"

"On Monday, December eighteenth. So, ten more days, which is way sooner than my liking. The place has a ways to go. In hindsight, I should've had Ruby do a walk-through for me so I could've been better prepared. But that is the least of my worries right now."

"What do you mean?" Ms. King took the tomatoes out of the pan and set them in a paper towel-lined colander to cool and drain.

I fidgeted. "There has been a mix up with the business space I rented from Coraline of Coraline's Classic Beauty Salon. It turns out I'm not the only one she leased the place to."

Ms. King paused in the act of sprinkling sea salt across the delicious smelling tomatoes. Her gaze flicked to mine. "I'm sorry, what?"

I groaned aloud. "Coraline is my landlady and she somehow leased the business space to both me, and to Dallas Parker. Do you remember him?"

Ms. King set the salt aside and reached for the pepper-shaker. "I do. He's pretty unforgettable." She went to the fridge and pulled out mayo and arugula. "You had a huge crush on him as I recall."

I twisted my lips. "Everyone keeps saying that." I reached for a potholder and carefully pulled the bread and bacon from the oven. I dabbed the top of the bread to make sure it was the proper level of crispiness while retaining its chewy interior. "And, yes, maybe it was true that I had a crush on Dallas. In fact, my feelings for him only seem to have grown."

"Well, then . . ." Ms. King set the mayo and lettuce on the counter and wiped her hands. Her knowing tone didn't sit well with me as I sliced the bread into thick sections while she washed the arugula. Then we layered the sandwiches together. Her eyes danced as she glanced over at me. "What's the problem with sharing a business space with Dallas?"

"You know my mom blames him for Grace's death." I sighed, finally admitting the truth as we sat down at the table to eat lunch. "I ignored my feelings for Dallas when we were young by avoiding him. Now that we've been forced to share the same space? We've grown closer than I ever thought possible."

I hadn't planned to fall for someone my mom could never accept, but that was exactly what had happened. I'd fallen for Dallas big time. I didn't want to hurt my mom. Unfortunately, it was only a matter of time until she found out about us.

Confiding in Ms. King had been comforting. She'd given me a warm smile, squeezed my hand, and said she was sure things would work out the way they were supposed to. It was simply amazing that a woman dying from kidney cancer could be so optimistic. She was that kind of person, though, one who made the world shine more brightly. I felt grateful to have had her in my life and I would miss her when she was gone.

CHAPTER NINE

The next day, Dallas and I worked for ten hours straight at our beauty salon slash furniture store. The floors were done, the antacid-orange chairs and tacky old gilt mirrors had been disassembled and donated, the walls were freshly painted, and the sagging old furniture that had sat in the front was now out of there, and the space was clean and shining.

There was still so much to do, though, and the tree, sitting in a metal holder, was next on our list. I'd taken down the dusty and dirty old blinds and strung lights around the windows but that naked tree wasn't looking too hot at the moment. I had run out of excuses with my parents to avoid them, but shockingly they hadn't contacted me all week.

I wondered if my mom had some Christmas volunteering obligation or if she was biding her time. Because she must've heard by now that I was staying with Ruby. But I didn't want to think about any of that at this moment. We'd already decorated Dallas's tree at his house, and the one I'd given to Ruby. Now, I wanted to decorate the tree for our businesses' window.

Dallas plucked a strand of trim out of one of the shopping

bags full of decorations we'd bought earlier today. "What, exactly, is this?" he asked.

I turned to look at him and my heart gave a soft flutter as I checked him out. He'd shucked the leather jacket. His long-sleeved shirt and jeans clung to his body in an appealing way. One of his eyebrows lifted as he stared at the strand of gold trim suspiciously. A warm feeling of love rolled through me.

I swallowed hard. "It goes around the tree. You can drape and wrap it and when you run out of that string then put another beside it so the whole strip looks like one piece."

A knock sounded on the front door and I jumped. Huh. Hadn't been expecting anyone. I peeked out the window to see who was there. A small frown creased my forehead. "Um, there's a delivery guy out there. Did you order something?" I asked.

Dallas tossed the strand of trim at the tree. It caught and hung on a branch. "Yep. Thought we could use some dinner after our hard work."

I smiled. "Aww, thanks."

"You're welcome." He headed for the door and dealt with the delivery person while I removed the trim so I could get it better situated. The smell of hot and gooey cheese, bacon, and olives hit my nose and I completely forgot about the trim and the tree as Dallas came inside with a pizza.

My belly rumbled. "That smells amazing."

He set the pizza box on a small table we'd set up to hold tools and things. He settled a six-pack of beer beside the box and I eyed the bottles. "The pizza place delivers beer?"

"It's actually a craft brewery that makes the best pizza in town. This is their pale ale."

"Huh." I headed for the table. "The place must be new."

Dallas twisted the tops off two beers and passed one to me.

I took a sip and the chilled liquid hit my throat, tasting like hops and malt. I swallowed. "Refreshing."

He lifted the top of the box and I stared down at the wood fired pie with delight. He handed me a paper plate. "Here you go."

"Thanks," I said, loving that he'd so casually taken care of dinner for us. We helped ourselves to the pizza and then went back to the tree with plates and beers in hand.

I stared at the tree, imagining how it would look all decorated. "This is going to draw in clients," I said, then sank my teeth into delicious gooey cheese and tomato sauce.

Dallas bit into a crispy-crusted slice and nodded. "Glad I talked you into it."

"I think you have that backwards." I gave him a sideways glance and watched him wink at me. Then I bit deep into the pizza again, sighing happily as the flavors of roasted garlic, red pepper, and cheese met my taste buds. I paused before taking another bite. "I was the one who suggested this particular tree."

"So you did." He winked at me, his eyes twinkling and my heart picked up to a rapid pulse. I'd been hoping we could talk about what was happening between us since I wasn't going to be able to force him out of the salon until Coraline returned Christmas Eve and I wasn't able to keep him out of my heart either.

It hit me then that we'd been spending so much time together with fun and easy banter—not to mention earth shattering kisses—but I didn't know much about his time between high school graduation and now. I set my plate down and picked up a box of bulbs then began threading the accompanying hooks through them while Dallas sipped his beer and then began settling the trim end to end to make a nice continuous loop around the bottom of the tree.

I knelt down beside him and wrapped my arm around his shoulder. "So... I have an awkward question for you."

"Maybe I can give you an awkward answer." He turned to me, the corners of his mouth lifting as he brushed his lips over mine. Oh, yum.

"Have you been dating anyone?" My cheeks heated as I realized how that sounded. "Not that I think you're dating anyone else right now. I mean, we're with each other all day long and it's not like you've snuck off to the other room to check your phone or anything." I rolled my eyes, wishing I could take back everything that had just spewed from my mouth. "The last girl I saw you with was Nina Abbott when she took you to her prom. You came back to town to go with her, so I'm just . . . curious about your love life," I said, and then took a long swig of beer. "I'm really good at this, aren't I?"

He chuckled, playing with the hair beside my cheek. "I've dated. Never that seriously, though."

"Why not?" I asked, trying to sound casual as I took an ornament from the bag and placed the blue and gold swirled ball on the tree right above the trim. Silence. I peeked over to see him standing there, a bulb resting on one palm.

He shrugged. "Didn't date much while I was in the military. After I got out, I met a woman I liked and for a while it was good. But I didn't see it going anywhere long-term."

Red flags flew up. "So you're commitment shy?"

"Where is all of this coming from?" He exchanged a look with me. When I didn't answer, he hooked the bulb on the tree. "She was a nice person. But it just . . . didn't seem right. She needed me to be there more and I couldn't be. Right around that time, my aunt got sick. I was so caught up coming back to visit her that I didn't have a lot left over. Then she didn't get better and I decided to move back to Christmas

Mountain," he said, lifting his beer to his lips and taking a swig.

He didn't have to say he hadn't asked her to come back with him. I already understood. He was, as Connor had said, the kind of guy who clammed up when things hurt. He had done that with that woman, which made me wonder how he'd be with me if things got hard.

I settled another bulb. "So you two broke up?"

"Yes, but we keep in touch on occasion."

I winced. "Do you miss her?"

"I feel bad about how we broke things off, but she wasn't the right person for me. She's married now and happy. I'm glad because she's a really good person." He paused again, then a line formed between his eyebrows. "How about you?"

Oops. I'd walked into that one.

I shrugged. "I've been busy for so long, trying to be the perfect daughter—the one my parents want me to be—that dating was usually the last thing on my mind. I'd date on occasion. But nobody special."

"Good," he said. His facial muscles softened as he gazed up at me, making me melt.

I ran my fingers through his short, dark hair, loving the soft feel beneath my fingertips. Eight years had passed by without us seeing each other and already I couldn't imagine what life would be like without him. "Do you see your uncle often?"

He nodded and then got to his feet, picking up a container of silvery tinsel. "He's over at Sunny Acres. It's supposed to be the best in the area and he has dedicated care there." He popped the tinsel container open. "Why do you try to be who your parents want you to be? At some point, you're going to have to live your own life. Right?"

Ouch. "If I were still trying, I'd have my MBA and be

working at their bank with Connor. Instead of being here doing this." But what was this? What was happening between us and would it last? Fresh worries set in. If this thing between us went sour then where would that leave us, especially if we were sharing a business space? "But I did what they wanted for a long time. I guess I didn't want to disappoint them or hurt them. I still don't want to. . . They're my parents. I love them."

Dallas took a seat in a chair. He dabbed at the water ring his bottle had left there but he didn't answer. I finished off my beer, wondering if he was thinking about his own parents—his mom who had left and his dad who still didn't have his life together.

I didn't know what they put in that pale ale. Liquid courage maybe, because I set my empty bottle down and took a seat right in his lap. I ran my fingers through the back of his hair. "You know you can trust me, right? We've known each other all our lives, so you know I'm not out to hurt you, right? Not ever."

"I should buy you pizza more often." There was laughter in his voice but a serious note hung below it and he slipped his arm around my waist, pulling me close to him. "I'm glad you came back, angel."

My heart melted. "Me, too." I had no idea if what was happening between us would last, but I wanted to find out. I gestured toward the tree. "We make a great decorating team."

His legs shifted under me. "I think we'll be a good team in the shop, too. That is, if you don't come up with some nefarious plot to get me tossed out."

My mouth fell open. How had he known what I was thinking? "You have to admit that a beauty salon and a furniture store doesn't seem like the best combination."

"You never know." He shrugged. "I can't believe you

decided to be a beautician. Come to think of it, you were always carrying a doll around. I remember one time you cut the hair off and cried when it didn't grow back."

"Yes, Miss Kitty Lee was devastated by her permanent crew cut when she wanted to grow it out again." I giggled, touched that he'd connected my passion to where it began. "How did you get into making furniture?" I asked.

He reached for a second beer, keeping one arm secure around my waist. "I made my first chair when I was a kid."

My eyebrows lifted. "I never heard you say anything about it back then."

His fingers tightened on my waist, sending heat flares skittering along my skin. "I know. I stopped for a long time. I was about eight years old the night I showed my folks the chair I made out of glue, leftover wood and a bed pillow. They laughed their heads off. I thought it was amazing at the time and they swore it was, but what was I thinking with a bed pillow?"

I fought back laughter. "It sounds like a good start."

He nodded. "I remember every minute of that night. I brought the chair out from the garage where I'd been working on it. My mom was cooking dinner. She stopped and said, 'that's beautiful, honey' when it had to be the ugliest chair ever made."

I smiled at him. "I'm sure it wasn't that bad."

"I used the pillow with a superhero pillowcase still on it."

I sputtered laughter. "But your mom loved it, right?"

He nodded. "She seemed so excited about it. She sat down in it and swore it was the most comfortable chair she'd ever sat in."

"Must've been the pillow," I said with a grin. "It had superhero power level comfort."

He roared laughter. "She called my dad in the kitchen and

he knelt down, checking the rungs and the pillow and then he declared it was perfect. He said next I should make a table that we could use in the dining room since ours was getting older."

I'd never seen Dallas come alive with so much energy. I hung on every word he said, especially since his dad had changed so much after his mom left.

"What happened next?" I asked, my body humming with anticipation.

He fidgeted. "Mom insisted on sitting in it and after dinner we had dessert. The next week, she packed her bags and left. She never came back."

My gut clenched. "Did she say why?"

"She and my dad had an argument, bigger than usual." A line formed between his brows. "But I didn't know that a mom could leave for good," he said, his voice catching in his throat. "Once, I asked my dad where she went and whether or not she'd return."

I waited for him to go on, but his jaw had tightened. "What did your dad say?"

His gaze met mine. "He said not to waste my time thinking about that woman."

"Ouch." My heart tightened with pain for him. "I'm sorry, Dallas."

He nodded slowly. "I've never told anyone that story before."

"Thanks for trusting me," I said, knowing how much that meant coming from someone who had been hurt by the ones he'd loved most. I also knew he took things to heart and had probably felt as much guilt over his mother's desertion as he did over his uncle's accident. I suspected his dad had a hand in the guilt Dallas felt. It wasn't fair. "My sister died," I blurted.

"I know, angel," he whispered.

Of course he did. He'd been there when it happened.

"Afterwards, my mom was so grief stricken," I said, my throat tightening as I shared what haunted me most. "She stayed in her room and rarely came out for meals. It went on for months. I never want to see her upset like that again. It's like I've become the replacement daughter, trying to be everything my mom thought Grace could've been. My parents were always so proud of her."

The corner of his mouth turned down. "You're an amazing person, Morgan. No matter what Grace might've accomplished, you have to live the life that's right for you. You can't try to replace someone who's gone. Nobody should expect that of you."

There was a haunted look in his eyes. Tears sprang into mine. I got up and walked over to the tree, my whole body shaking. "I know that on one level." My voice was hoarse. "But I want to be enough for my folks. I'm the only daughter they have and part of me wants to be more than that, to fill that hole Grace left . . ." My fingers went to a pile of ornaments I'd painted earlier with Ruby's leftover paints. I picked one up at random and held it as he came over to me.

"Morgan—"

"I just wish . . ." Tears clouded my vision and made everything blurry. "That night had never happened. That Grace was still with us. Mom never talks about her unless she's pointing out something I'm doing wrong."

I guided the ornament to the tree and hooked it on a sturdy branch to let the blue-eyed angel with the rosy lips dangle there. She reminded me of my sister. Angels always reminded me of Grace. I lifted another angel ornament from a bag.

Dallas looped his arms around my waist. I turned toward him, intending to say something, but instead I kissed him. He tasted like a combination of pizza and ale and *him*. His firm lips parted against mine and he tasted me. Oh, yum.

My pulse raced along, faster and faster, and I forgot about everything, the worries I had about my folks and the salon as my arms went round his neck and I leaned into that kiss with everything in me. The tears spilling over my cheeks salted our kiss but he held me tight, kissing away the sad past and bringing me into the present moment.

"Morgan Reed," came a familiar female voice, jerking me from my heavenly fog. The two words were firm, like a warning without even raising her tone.

Dallas broke off the kiss so fast that it left me breathless as my head swiveled toward the front door and the woman who stood there. My heart dropped like a rock straight to my belly.

I managed to squeak out, "Mom?"

My mom stood inside the doorway, her dark-brown hair elegantly coiffed in a simple French twist, thick lash extensions framing her green eyes, and her trim body neatly attired in an elegant pair of slacks and a white cashmere sweater.

She advanced a few steps. "What is going on here?"

Her tone indicated bewilderment and disapproval, the kind of tone she used when something didn't meet Ivy Reed's standards or approval.

That something being me.

CHAPTER TEN

The ornament in my hand gave off a small rattle as my hands began to tremble. My mom advanced further into the space and my gaze flew out the window to the Cadillac Escalade parked right in front. I hadn't seen her SUV pull up. But I'd been so absorbed in Dallas and the tree and our soul-baring conversation.

My mom tilted her head. "Dallas Parker. I'd heard you were back."

Her voice gave new meaning to the word "frosty" as she spoke to him and it was a wonder the window didn't gain an inch of ice. I gulped and eyed the distance to the stockroom, which had a back door. I considered making a run for it, but I knew that—despite the fact that she wore sharply heeled boots—she'd be willing and able to chase me down.

When Ivy Reed was determined to have something then nothing stopped her. Besides, my mom wore heels like most women wore perfume. She could probably run a marathon in those things and never feel a single ounce of calf strain. Scary, but impressive.

"Hello, Mrs. Reed." Dallas nodded to her and appeared at

ease, but I could see the vein on his temple throbbing. He brushed a gleam of moisture from his bottom lip, which had obviously been put there by me. Oops.

"Funny story," I said, managing to speak through the rock in my throat. I was in so much trouble they needed to invent a new word for trouble. "Dallas and I somehow managed to lease the same business space. Isn't that crazy?"

Her eyes narrowed. "I beg your pardon?"

"The landlady rented the space to both of us," Dallas said.

"Sounds like a legal issue." Mom's eyebrows drew together as I eased the angel ornament onto the tree, hoping the angel would bring me good luck. "I suppose that explains what you're doing here with *him*. Besides the obvious, that is."

My face heated big time. Getting caught kissing a guy would've been bad enough. Getting caught kissing Dallas Parker? That might necessitate having to leave town. "I've become aware that Morgan is opening a beauty salon. But if the sign outside is any indication, you're selling used furniture on consignment, Dallas?"

My gut clenched and my gaze flew to Dallas. It had been a lot of years since he'd decked Tom Brand, but part of me worried he might lash out at my mom's condescending tone. And that would so *not* improve my situation. Luckily, his face looked neutral.

"I build the furniture myself," he said, simply.

"Interesting," she said, surveying the shop. A moment ago I'd felt like our hard work was visible but now I could only see what hadn't been done, including our half-decorated tree.

"We still have a lot to do obviously," I said, my voice trembling. I watched disappointment flood her face, sending a slice of pain to my heart. She was disappointed in my salon. She was disappointed in me. I'd never be the daughter she really wanted. Tears threatened. I needed to get busy to keep them at bay. "Speaking of having a lot to do, I'd better finish decorating our tree."

Mom peered at one of the branches. "Is that tinsel?"

She'd said "tinsel" like it was a dirty word.

I regarded the silvery strands. "Yes."

"Oh, my. I didn't think I knew anyone who'd actually put that stuff on their tree. It's so tacky, and it gets into everything." She scanned the tree, her gaze stopping mid-point. She reached toward a bulb. "This one is off-center." She tweaked it slightly. "You also have two reds next to each other and too many greens next to the golds."

I stood there, irritated as she began rearranging the bulbs. No matter that I'd liked them the way they were. . . .

She glanced at me as she worked. "I'm disappointed you haven't made time to visit your father and me, Morgan. You seem to be over the illness that suddenly struck you."

"I'm sorry, but I've been so busy." I grabbed the cardboard box that held the tinsel and began yanking thick clumps of it out. I draped the tinsel over the tree limbs and Mom immediately began to pluck it off as I went. "Sweetie, if you have to use tinsel do it sparingly, like so." She left one single strand hanging and then blocked it from view with a gingerbread house ornament.

"Mrs. Reed?" Dallas called out, making me cringe. I'd been hoping she'd forgotten he was here and that he'd had her daughter in a lip-lock earlier, but it was harder to stay in denial with him talking aloud. "I could use a different perspective on this sofa. I tend to build for comfort, but perhaps this needs more style. What do you think?"

He was trying to help, to lessen her focus on me and give me room to gather my thoughts. I was grateful for his attempt to help but it didn't do much good. My mom's fingers hovered above a red bulb, which was decorated with a flurry of white snowflakes. "It's not my style, but I suppose I wouldn't be shocked if it sold. Everyone seems to want *modern* nowadays."

She managed to make "modern" sound like a dirty word, too, when I knew good and well the painting she'd purchased on our Caribbean cruise fit the definition.

Irritation rolled through me. "Dallas makes beautiful furniture in many different styles. I think his entire store is going to be a hit."

Dallas shook his head slowly, telling me to leave it alone. But my comment had been like a reflex. I couldn't stand up for myself, but I wouldn't stand for her picking on him.

My mom gave me a tired look. She fingered the trim Dallas had settled along the branches, wrinkling her nose at it. "I don't know how you can have a beauty salon and a furniture store in the same location. This seems to be the most unlikely pairing I've ever seen."

Her gaze flew to Dallas as she spoke, leaving no doubt that she meant more than the store by her comment. My irritation grew.

"I think it's a terrific pairing," I said, gesturing around the room, which, admittedly, still needed a whole lot of work. "Look how that table accents the wood floor. Dallas laid the hardwood himself, saving us labor costs. And I don't think I've ever seen such beautiful floors, or such a stunning table. You should see his house, too. The furniture he made for it is incredible. I loved everything in there."

Oops. I cringed. What were the chances my mom wouldn't catch what I'd just admitted? I watched her eyes narrow. Yeah, that would be slim to none. Gulp.

She pulled more tinsel off the tree and placed it back into the cardboard box. "You have time to visit Dallas at his home, but not time for your father or me?"

Guilt settled deep in my bones, thick and smothering. I

knew I was wrong for not telling them about the salon or going to see them right away. But I'd had my reasons and the main one was staring me in the face at that very second. I mean, this was exactly the scenario I'd been hoping to avoid.

My mom was so controlling she couldn't even let me decorate my own Christmas tree! I yanked the tinsel box up off the table and pulled the stuff out again. I tossed a bunch of strands at the tree, my nerves so shattered all I could do was try to regain control over some part of the situation and my life. Granted, tinsel wasn't the best solution—and the amount I'd thrown on did seem on the tacky side—but I piled more on anyway.

Dallas cleared his throat. "I'll leave you two to talk privately."

"What a wonderful idea," my mom said.

"No . . ." I started, but my voice trailed off because he'd already turned and gone. The traitor. He was out the door before I could even frame a protest, much less utter an intelligent reason why I shouldn't be left alone in the room with my own mother.

Mom waited three seconds. "Do I need to list the reasons why I'm upset?"

"No, I can guess." I rubbed my hands over my face, sucking in a deep breath. "I'm sorry I lied about how I spent my trust fund. I should've told you I didn't want an MBA, but . . . *no*, no excuses. I should've at least told you the minute I arrived in town."

She smoothed a set of crystal icicles on the tree and sniffed. "I'm worried about you."

Okay, I hadn't expected that one. "Why?"

"You're not acting like the Morgan I know." She turned to me and I could see the worry in her eyes. "I love Christmas. I enjoyed that cruise last year but, well, Miami isn't home. Is it?

I'd hoped you'd come home this year. And you did. But you didn't want to see me."

"It's not that I didn't want to see you." I stepped toward her, tears threatening to choke me. "One of the reasons I returned home was because I missed you and Dad and Connor. I've wanted to come back for years, but I didn't want to work at the bank. I want this," I said, gesturing around me, which didn't look all that impressive. "Well, not in its current state. But the salon will be amazing when I'm done with it."

Her hands flew to her hips. "Morgan Reed, you simply cannot open and run a beauty salon. Think of your education. What a waste. How would you use it?"

Okay, that was more the reaction I'd expected.

"To run a profitable business," I retorted. "To make sure I increase my savings, so I can buy a home. I can think of a thousand ways to use my degree practically in life."

She blew out a breath and patted her cheeks, obviously trying to compose herself. Then she got distracted by something over my shoulder. Suddenly, she knelt and tugged at the green felt at the base of the tree to hide the small inch of metal holder exposed. "It's not just that you lied about how you spent your inheritance. Although that does trouble me. You're using the funds for something that your grandparents never intended. The trust was set up for your education. If you stop this madness, your dad could probably reinvest whatever you have left and help you recoup your losses. I think that's the best idea."

My fists balled at my sides. "Grandma and Grandpa never put a single stipulation on what Connor and I could do with our trusts. I'm opening this salon and I'm going to be a beautician." The words roared out of my mouth, shattering the hush that had gathered in the store.

Mom twisted her fingers together. "I know you think this is

what you want, but the bank would be so much better for you. You'd have a stable career there. You spent four years at the university learning what you'd need to be successful at the bank. You'd be working with your father, and helping to maintain this family's legacy. I'm sure you want that."

I took three fiery breaths, so I wouldn't explode. "No, I don't want that. You're not even listening to me. I have the right to live my life in a way that will make me happy. You think you know what's best for me, but I don't want to work at the bank and I won't. Ever."

Her mouth opened in a shocked expression and an apology flew to my lips, but I held it back. I didn't want to hurt her, or disappoint her, but at some point I had to live my life. I'd been miserable for so long. Now that I'd figured out how happy I could be, there was no way I wanted to lose that or my soul would shrivel up and die.

She held her palms up in that stop gesture I'd known my entire life. "How can you say these things to me? You've always wanted to work in the bank. Ever since you were young you wanted that."

I shook my head. "I always wanted to be a cosmetologist. Don't you remember how I used to play with dolls? I used to cut their hair, or curl it, or paint their nails, and I'd sneak your makeup to put it on them."

Her face went the same color as curdled milk. "This rebellion of yours, or whatever it is, just needs to stop. Connor works at the bank. Grace would've worked at the bank. You will work at the bank like your brother and sister."

Everything inside me crumbled. Her words about how Grace would've worked in the bank knocked me like a punch to my gut. Right behind that hurt came that heavy mantle of guilt. Guilt that I'd lived and that she had died. That I couldn't measure up. That I didn't know how to be the daughter she would've been.

The feeling of guilt was so complex and multi-layered and it hit me then that that guilt was the real reason I'd stayed in Miami for so long. Nobody there knew about my sister. Nobody had ever known my sister and had no way to compare me to her.

That guilt and the hurt and the anger that always ran below those things made me snap, "Why can't you ever see *me*? Why do you always have to see Grace in everything that I do?"

Mom licked her lips. Her hand came up and patted at her hair. "I see you're too upset to talk about this now and I am as well. We're having dinner at the club tomorrow night. Your father, Connor, and I will be there. It's our usual dinner night. It would be nice if you would attend so that we could discuss this in a more civilized manner as a family."

In other words, be there. Or else. There was no way to say no to such a guilt-heavy thing. I knew it and she knew that I knew it. It was Ivy Reed's classic mom calling card. I sighed. "Okay. I'll be there."

Mom nodded briskly. "Good. Seven o'clock sharp."

"I'll be there at seven," I said, sighing again. Okay, I'd kept things from her, which wasn't nice. But when had I ever not been punctual?

Her expression softened. "I love you, sweetheart."

Even though I felt like a truck had run over me, I forced a weak smile. "I love you, too."

She did love me. But she had loved Grace more.

"Good night then." She left and I turned to stare at the tree. Tears blurred my vision again and this time I let those tears slide down my cheeks.

Of course the tree looked fabulous the way my mom had

rearranged it. Christmas was my mom's favorite holiday and she'd always saved decorating the tree for last because she took so much real pleasure in it. The only activity she loved more was setting the table. She approached both decorating the tree and those table settings with the same eye to beauty and elegance and it showed at that moment.

Past the Christmas tree the streetlights glowed and I could see that they'd set up the booth where Santa would sit to listen to kids whisper their Christmas wishes. Back when I'd been small I'd always asked for the same thing every year. For Santa to bring my sister back, so my mom wouldn't be sad anymore. So she would have the daughter she really wanted and then I could walk my own path instead of attempting to fill Grace's shoes.

Shoes I'd never be able to fill if I tried for the rest of my life.

CHAPTER ELEVEN

Late the next day, Dallas and I strolled away from downtown and up the stairs to The Sharing Tree that stood next to Kissing Bench beside the Falls. The Sharing Tree had been there for as long as I could remember, a tall tree with a wide body furred with green needles and long green branches, which were the perfect length for decorating.

And the town did decorate The Sharing Tree, every single year. The whole town got together and turned that tree into a kind of Christmas Mountain mascot, looking like a gloriously bedecked creation that screamed Christmas cheer and joy. Couples would hang ornaments to pledge their love and others would also hang ornaments in remembrance of a loved one.

There was nobody else there at the moment, though. Dallas and I stood beside the tree on that cold windy Saturday afternoon, watching the tree's branches flutter and listening to the melodic notes of the ornaments jingling, a counterpoint to the rushing sound of the Falls.

"You ready?" Dallas asked, slipping his arm around me.

"Yes." I nodded and looked down at the angel ornament I

held, which I planned to put on the tree. The angel had dark hair, blue eyes, and a rose mouth, reminding me of my big sister.

Every year after Grace had died, I'd hung an angel in remembrance of her. Usually, I'd buy an angel ornament while shopping downtown. This year, I'd painted my own angel for her at Ruby's townhome. The family dinner at the country club tonight loomed over my head and that argument with my mom clouded everything between Dallas and me.

"Watch your step," he said, his hand settling below my arm to steady me as I wobbled. "It's slick here. There's dew on the rocks which has frozen."

His words stopped me in my tracks, stirring something from my memory. It had been *slick* the day of Grace's accident. I hadn't watched my step. Every muscle in my body went rigid and I found myself reliving that awful accident in my mind.

Grace had been the oldest child in our family, a few years ahead of Connor. Mom had put her in charge of us that afternoon when we invited Ruby and Dallas over to play. But it had been Dallas who'd talked us into leaving the house when we were supposed to stay home. He'd suggested we go for a nature walk, and where better to go than the Falls?

I gulped as the memories flooded into my head. I hadn't been watching where I'd been skipping on that nature walk, just followed the others merrily as we hiked up the back of the Falls. I'd been having such fun with Ruby and Grace and Connor. Plus, my eyes had been glued on Dallas, who I'd had the beginnings of a crush on even at seven.

I was so close to the edge of the cliff as we went and should've been paying attention to where I was walking. But I'd flapped about and slipped on the slick granite beneath my feet.

My stomach dropped as I started falling over the edge....

"Morgan?" Dallas asked, jerking me back to the present. I could hear the Falls crashing beside us with its gentle roar. He slipped his hand around mine and squeezed. "You okay?"

"I don't know," I lied, but I did know. I wasn't all right. Not even close. How could I be? I'd lived with this guilt for so long now—from what I'd never told another soul.

"You're thinking about Grace." It was a statement, not a question.

"Yes." I nodded, but it was more than that. My lips trembled. Everything in my childhood up to that point had been golden and rosy. I'd never told anyone the truth about why everything had changed. But staring into his gentle caramel-brown eyes, I knew it was time to be honest. "The accident was *my* fault. Grace died because of me."

"What are you talking about?" he said, softly.

"I-I should've been more careful that day." My vision blurred. I closed my eyes, transporting myself back in time as a hot tear slid down my cheek. "I slipped, Dallas. I started falling backward. I would've gone over the cliff. It all happened so fast. But I can still feel Grace's hand on my arm, yanking me back toward safety. And when I turned around she wasn't behind me anymore. She'd gone over the edge."

His gaze held mine, but there was no blame in them.

"If I'd been watching where I was going then Grace would still be alive," I said, trying to make him understand. After finally admitting that aloud, the weight of my guilt lifted off my shoulders, replaced by a sorrow so strong that it threatened to crush me. My knees buckled. "She'd still be alive."

I dropped down onto the cement and sobs escaped in loud racking bursts. A gaping hole burst through my chest, leaving me open and vulnerable. Grace had died saving me, because I hadn't been careful. It was my fault. In the depth of my pain, warm hands cupped my cheeks.

"Listen to me." Dallas's voice was gentle, but firm as he lifted my face to his. "You told me that accident with my uncle wasn't my fault and I had to let it go—"

"This is different," I snapped, staring at him. Didn't he get that this was different? I swallowed hard, fighting for breath. "If I'd been paying attention then Grace wouldn't have died."

"If I'd set my alarm then my uncle wouldn't have suffered that injury."

I shook my head. "You don't know that. There are too many variables. The accident could've happened anyway . . ." My voice trailed off as my own words hit me.

"Is there anything you wouldn't have done to save her?" he whispered, his thumbs brushing my cheeks.

"No," I said, my voice coming out in a hiccup, before my breathing started to slow down.

"Me, either." He dropped his forehead to mine. "You have to let go of the guilt. We both do."

I laced my arms around him, burying my nose into his neck. I breathed in slowly. He smelled like lumber. His scent made me feel warm and safe, like I wasn't alone. We were a team.

"My mom blames you for Grace's death." I murmured, letting him pull me closer against his firm chest.

"I know." He pulled back and sighed. "Many times I've felt that way, too. If I hadn't suggested the nature walk—"

"We all wanted to go," I said, sniffling and rubbing my nose. "Grace did, too. You were always the fun one in our group." A smile came to my lips. Then out of the corner of my eye, I spotted a couple coming up the stairs. Dallas stood, pulling me up with him. A minute later, they passed by us and took a seat on Kissing Bench, cuddling and looking very much in love. So sweet. After talking with Dallas, I felt lighter, but drained. And the day wasn't over yet. "I'm having dinner at the club with the parents tonight."

He smirked. "I hear the food's good there."

I shot him a sidelong glance. "Is that an idle comment or are you hoping to come along?"

"I'm just saying." His grin became wide and toothy. He lifted my hand, swinging it back and forth. "And no way am I going to that dinner without a proper invitation. Your mom scares me. And I was in the Marines, so that's saying something."

My smile was rueful. "Yeah, she can be scary. I feel like she doesn't mean to be, though. She only wants to . . . control everything and everyone." I laughed, bitterly. "But it comes from a good place. She thinks she's doing what's best."

"After what happened with Grace, I shouldn't have done so much crazy stuff with Connor. She was probably scared I'd get another one of her kids killed." His hand rested on my shoulder, the touch light but very much there. "Even if your mom has some faults, at least she's still there for you."

His words gave me a chill. "You're right. I can't imagine what it would be like not to have a mother," I said, softly.

He glanced away, looking at The Sharing Tree and wearing a pained expression. His shoulders lifted and dropped like he wanted to shrug that comment off. "She left a hole that can never be filled."

"I'm sorry, Dallas." I shook my head. My sister's death had left a hole in our lives, too, but she hadn't *chosen* to leave us. I couldn't imagine the hole his mom had created. "I'm sure your mom had problems. But I wish she'd made a different choice—for your sake and for hers. She missed out being with you, too."

"My mom loved Christmas." He gestured to The Sharing Tree. "She'd decorate this tree and the one at home. Every year, she'd buy gingerbread houses and we'd put them together. My dad would eat the roofs and steal the icing, acting like a kid." He chuckled at the memory. "Once, he ate a gingerbread bridge made from plastic."

My hand flew to my mouth. "How did that work out?"

"After the trip to the emergency room or before?" He grinned, showing merriment at first and then his smile faded. He tucked a piece of my stray hair behind my ear. "I miss those times."

"It's weird how life goes on." I took in his sad expression, my mind moving back to Grace. "It seems like everyone has forgotten that Grace died on the other side of the Falls. Sometimes I wish there was some kind of marker to let people know she'd been there. I visit her gravesite sometimes, but I'd rather think of her in a place where she'd been alive."

He turned away from me, looking up toward the top of the Falls. "I could build a bench and put it back there, so you could go and sit anytime you want."

I blinked at him. "You'd do that for me?"

"Yes," he said, his eyebrows coming together in a way that said that shouldn't even be a question. "I'd even sit there with you."

I threw my arms around him in an impulsive hug, and pressed my cheek to his chest. We stayed that way in each other's arms for a long time. Then my eyes drifted to the bench that the couple just vacated. I thought of the night he'd punched my boyfriend and still wondered what that had been about. I opened my mouth to ask him—

Before I could speak, he kissed me.

The kiss caught me off guard and took my breath way. My hands pressed against his chest as I kissed him back. The steady thrum of his heartbeat beneath his shirt and coat felt reassuring. I forgot about that night with Tom and the question I'd been about to ask, especially as our kiss turned heated, warming me and keeping the late afternoon chill at bay.

We finally broke apart. I smiled up at him. His mouth curved upward in return.

"I'm ready to hang this angel ornament for Grace." I looked down at the small angel still in my grip. "When I do this, it makes me feel like an angel is watching over my sister. Maybe the angel will watch over your mom, too, wherever she is."

"You have the biggest heart I know," he said, the tender expression in his eyes making me melt. He smiled as his fingers closed over mine.

Then we reached forward together, hanging the sweet angel on the highest limb we could reach. When I looked up at her, I could almost feel her smiling.

CHAPTER TWELVE

The country club sat on a high rise of hill, tucked back among acres of pine and old fir trees. The building, low and rambling, had been built to blend in with nature and so the cedar siding and shingles made it seem like the place had grown up on that spot.

All of the windows sent out a warm amber light, there were small twinkling lights along the roofline, and the pine trees that lined the driveway had been decorated for Christmas. The white lights and bright star toppers glowed and would've made me smile if it weren't for my major uneasiness about how this "family" dinner would go.

I parked my car, hopped out, and hurried along the low ledge of sidewalk that fronted the building since I was running a little late. Oops! A red-and-black uniformed doorman opened the door and ushered me in with a smile. As I walked in, a rush of warm air hit me along with the lovely sound of "Silver Bells" playing softly from the speakers.

The lobby boasted stunning leather sofas for those waiting for a table and plush chairs sat in cozy groupings close to the floor-to-ceiling stone fireplace. Beside the crackling fire, sat a towering tree decorated with twinkling lights and surrounded by piles of exquisitely wrapped boxes bearing perfectly tied red ribbons.

The hostess, an older red-haired woman named Elizabeth who'd been there forever, greeted me. "Hello, Morgan. Your mother said you'd be joining the family this evening. They're already seated at their usual table. I'll take you there."

"Thank you." I nodded, feeling uneasy already.

As I followed her out of the lobby, I caught a glimpse of my reflection in a mirror. I'd taken great pains with my outfit: a long sleeved cashmere dress in an electric blue hue, tall, high-heeled boots, and diamond earrings. I'd blown my hair out after a good shampoo and gloss rinse, and then applied a careful amount of makeup, plus a fringe of eyelash extensions to give my eyes an additional pop. It occurred to me I'd taken so much time with my hair and makeup to show my mom how good I was at those things.

I spotted my mom, my dad, and Connor at a table tucked into a corner that had windows, which overlooked both the surrounding hills and the sparkling shimmer of downtown's lights and decorations. The dining table was covered with a fine white cloth, the napkins sat in china holders and the place settings were gold-rimmed.

I sucked in a breath as I approached. "Hi, everyone."

"Morgan!" Dad stood and gave me a big hug. The familiar scent of his cologne and the rustle of his evening clothes—a solid black jacket and pants, a crisp shirt smelling of starch and a festive red-and-blue striped tie—brought back so many memories. "You look so good, sweetheart. I'm happy to see you, even if you did hide out on us for a while."

Eek! I cringed, giving him a genuine smile. "I'm sorry about that, Dad."

Mom stood and gave me a stiff hug that said she hadn't

forgotten our argument. Her perfume was the same brand she had worn since I was a child and her hair was up and off her face, held back by elegant clips that had a small row of pearls on them. She wore matching pearl earrings and a single strand of pearls around her neck that contrasted beautifully with her black long-sleeve wool dress. "I love your dress, Morgan. Did we buy that the last time you were home?"

She knew very well I hadn't been home in eight years.

"No, you gave it to me last Christmas," I said, even though she knew I'd never wear this dress in Florida. I'd worn it tonight to show her I appreciated her. But she was already driving me nuts. I may as well have worn jeans and my "I do hairdos" top.

Connor gave me a hug and muttered into my ear, "If you have to face the firing squad then you might as well dress up for it so you leave a good looking corpse."

I sucked back a laugh and took my seat, taking the napkin out of the holder and laying it across my lap while I studied my family carefully.

The server came to our table and I stared at her familiar face. She was beautiful, lean, and tall, with flawless latte skin. Nina Abbott. She'd been in my grade at school, was an avid skier, and—oh, yeah—she'd taken Dallas to prom.

"Good evening . . ." Her voice trailed off as her eyes widened with recognition. "Oh, Morgan! You're back. It's great to see you again."

"Good to see you, too." I smiled at Nina, who had to have been close to Dallas for him to fly back for her prom. A picture of them dancing close at prom popped in my head. My stomach roiled at the image of him with another girl, even though prom was a long time ago. Nina had always been a nice girl and it wasn't her fault she and I had liked the same guy. "I think the last time I saw you was when I decided to take up snowboarding and you gave me a few lessons."

Connor chuckled. "Was that the year you slid down the mountain on your face?"

I shot him a glare. "Thanks for that, bro."

Nina smiled. "Morgan was doing quite well until that skier bowled her over."

I gave her a grateful look. I'd fallen more than I'd actually snowboarded, in truth, but it was nice to have an ally. "Thanks. I did sort of go down hard."

She flashed me a gentle smile. "Everyone does their first time. Do you still snowboard?"

I shook my head. "I've been living in Miami the last eight years. But your lessons did help me learn how to surf more easily."

Connor nudged me with his hand. "That sounds like a hard life, sis. All sea and sun and surfing."

I lifted an eyebrow at him. He grinned back at me. Then Nina took our orders and left.

Dad leaned back in his chair, fingering his chin. "Morgan, your mom told me about the place you rented downtown. Are you serious about this whole hair cutting thing?"

"Of course she isn't," Mom said.

I stiffened. Oh, great. It had started.

"She's serious enough to sink her money into a business," Connor said, coming to my rescue. "I'd say she's thought long and hard about opening the C.M. Salon."

Aww. He'd remembered the initials and hadn't even made fun of me. I'd give my brother an extra big hug later. "Thanks, bro," I said, gratefully.

"It seems so out of character for you," Dad said, looking utterly baffled as if I'd taken on a job as a belly dancer or something.

Nina returned, carefully placing a breadbasket and serving a white wine, before checking to see if we needed anything else before she left again.

I reached for a piping hot roll and buttered it generously.

Mom reached for her wine, giving me a sudden smile. "I meant to tell you that Thomas Brand stopped by our table before you arrived at *quarter past seven*." Her tone lowered on the last part, making it clear she'd noticed my tardy arrival. "He's in town for the holidays and enjoyed an early dinner with his grandparents. He asked after you."

"That's nice." I sank my teeth into the soft bread and creamy fresh butter, chewing slowly as my mom waited for a better reaction. She wasn't going to get one from me. Did she honestly think I'd trade Dallas for an ex-boyfriend because he happened to be back in town? Tom had dumped me for no reason and I'd been long over him.

Mom turned to gaze out the windows. "Do you remember the first time we brought you here, Morgan? After we'd joined the club?"

My chest went tight. "Yeah, I was nine."

Dad spoke over the rim of his wineglass. "You were so determined to be proper. You sat so still I was shocked you didn't freeze up and stay like that forever."

I took a huge gulp of wine. "I wanted to be such a good daughter."

"You always were honey. You and Grace were the best . . ." She stopped and looked away, her eyes going to the windows. "She would've loved the club so much. She used to beg to borrow my clear lip gloss because she thought it was lipstick. I can't imagine why she thought she needed lipstick for us to join the club, but it was so sweet . . ."

She fell silent. The muted sounds of the club hung around us: conversations and laughter, the chink of glasses and dishes and silverware, and Christmas carols in the background.

I shifted uneasily in my seat as Nina appeared and served our dinners. My stomach rolled as I looked down at the sea bass I'd ordered. It had looked amazing on the menu and looked amazing on the plate, but I had zero appetite.

"Do those peas have mint in them?" Connor asked.

I nodded. "That's what the menu said."

He dug his fork into my peas.

I lifted an eyebrow. "Why didn't you just order your own?"

He grinned at me around the mouthful of pilfered food. "I wanted the potatoes."

I rolled my eyes at him and then stuck my fork into his Yukon potatoes, taking a heap of creamy buttery potatoes. "I would've ordered my own. But, you know."

Dad chuckled. "You two. You always loved stealing food off each other's plates."

Mom laughed and it sounded genuine, making me smile. I popped the potatoes in my mouth, starting to relax for the first time this evening.

Then Mom lifted her wineglass. "I was thinking about Morgan's salon issue. Sweetheart, you said the landlady accidentally leased the space to both you and Dallas Parker. But what would happen if she came back and decided to give the lease to him?"

Just like that whatever appetite I'd mustered up had vanished. I set my fork and knife down. "I don't know," I said, answering honestly.

Dad pointed a finger in my direction. "She should refund your money. This double-lease situation was hardly your fault."

I didn't want my money back. I wanted my salon and I wanted it to be successful.

Mom nodded. "I still think it would be better to cut your losses here and now. Perhaps Dallas would give you back a portion given that he'll be taking over the space entirely. Then, you could come work at the bank and be with family and not have to worry about your income fluctuating and so on. You're twenty-six now. It's time to start thinking of buying your first home and settling down." She smiled as if the matter had been settled. "I do hope you'll see Tom while he's in town," she said, and the meaning was *not* lost on me.

"I doubt it." My gut churned. I managed to flake a bite of fish away from its bones and put it in my mouth, but I could taste nothing.

Connor touched my arm. "Well, I don't care if you choose to be a beautician, a banker, or a butcher, Morgan. I'm glad you're home."

Dad nodded. "I agree. It is nice to have the whole family together again."

Mom looked down at her plate a moment. "Yes, it's good to have you home, sweetheart," she said, her voice soft and sad.

I noticed she hadn't repeated, "the whole family was back together." Of course she would never say that. Grace wasn't here and so our family would never be whole again.

And that was my fault.

"It was time to come home," I said, as exhaustion set in. I'd known coming home would be hard. That opening my own salon was something I'd have to fight for and that it would be a hard fight. I just hadn't realized how hard it would actually be.

CHAPTER THIRTEEN

The next week flew by in a blur from all of the hours decorating the salon, stocking all of the supplies, and avoiding my mom's jabs about signing the lease over to Dallas each time I saw her. All of a sudden it was the Friday before my grand opening. Christmas was right around the corner and definitely in the air, too. The sidewalks were packed with shoppers and people peering at the decorative window displays downtown.

I'd picked up several "hairstyle" books at the bookstore earlier in the day and had run into Carol Bennett—one of my bff bracelet buddies from my choir team—who now worked there full-time. We caught up a bit on what we'd been up to since graduation. Apparently she'd been modeling all over the world, but had stopped because it was too high-pressure. She seemed happy to be at the bookstore, though.

One of the best things about being back in Christmas Mountain was seeing my old friends again. So I was definitely excited when Ruby invited me Christmas shopping.

"There's the shop I was telling you about the other day," Ruby said, as we came up to a store with a red and silver awning. "Moxie just opened. Anyway, let's look in here for the Secret Santa present I need for my gift exchange at work."

"Sounds good." I smiled, my feet slowing on the sidewalk as I took in the adorable window display that held a series of gift boxes wrapped neatly in red paper and green bows. "Dallas and I just added faux gifts under the tree in our store window," I said.

"Things are still going well between you two?" she asked, watching me nod. "Maybe you guys will exchange real gifts this year then, instead of just empty boxes under the tree at work."

"Very funny," I said, thinking we were too early in our relationship for gifts. Then my gaze fell on an item in the corner of the window display and an idea came to mind. "Actually, I think I will get Dallas a present."

"Huh. That was easy." Ruby opened the door and we walked through it. "Speaking of your shop. . . Are you ready for your grand opening? It's on Monday, right?"

"Yes." My heart gave off a massive thump. "I think we're ready. I hope so. But I always think that right before something breaks, or a pipe bursts, or the flooring decides to shift. Things tend to go wonky on me. Ahem, orange chair." I raised my eyebrows, exchanging a smirk with her. "What if something goes wrong?"

She waved a hand dismissively. "Don't beg for trouble."

"Right." I sighed, eyeing Moxie's Christmas tree and the kids gathered around it, all of them smiling and laughing as their parents shopped.

Suddenly, I imagined several small caramel-brown eyed kids gathered around a decorated tree on Christmas Eve. Dallas would have chopped it down himself, of course. We'd set the tree up beside his window with those incredible mountain views. He'd bring me a latte from Sleigh Café, we'd place an angel on top of the tree, and then we'd kiss, while our kids danced around us. . . .

"Look at that scarf. Is that cashmere?" Ruby asked.

I blinked, dragged from my thoughts. Had I really just imagined a future with Dallas? Talk about getting ahead of myself. Our relationship was only in the beginning stage. Although, we had known each other all of our lives. My stomach tightened. Christmas Eve was my family's special night to exchange thoughtful gifts, but my mom would *never* spend a holiday with Dallas Parker. She could barely look at him the one time she'd seen him. Sigh.

"It *is* cashmere." Ruby ran her fingers down the men's scarf and nodded as she held the soft pewter scarf out to examine it further. "Do you think my manager would like this?"

I nodded. "Um, yeah. But isn't that kind of an expensive gift for a Santa exchange? I always receive a bottle of wine or one of those tins filled with popcorn."

Ruby let the scarf go. "Do you think it's too much?"

"Not if there's something going on between you and your manager that you're not telling me," I said, raising my brows.

"Well, he has asked me out. But I'm not sure if I like him in that way . . ." Her voice trailed off, making me wonder what she was thinking about. Or, rather, *who*.

"Hmm." I decided not to prod further and headed toward a sign advertising gingerbread houses. When we got to the table itself, though, it was bare but for a few display houses. "Oh, no. I was hoping to get Dallas a gingerbread house kit. I wonder if they have any in the back?"

Ruby looked around but the two salesclerks were busy ringing people up, or running to the back to get something. "Give them a minute and we'll ask. Why do you want a gingerbread house kit? They're so hard to make."

"I know." I turned away from the table and examined a

table filled with gift sets. "I want to make a gingerbread house with Dallas. His mom used to make them with him when he was younger and he loved the tradition. I don't think he's made one since she left."

Ruby stopped poking through the gift sets. Her mouth dropped open. "Okay, *wow*. Making a gingerbread house is a commitment. They're crazy difficult and they can go down in a heap of crumbles and icing if you make one mistake. You don't make something with that potential for disaster unless you're committed to a man. So spill. Now."

I darted a glance around the store then grabbed her by the arm and guided her toward a quiet corner. I took a deep breath. "He took me to the Overlook last night. I love how amazing the view of town is from up there. All of the twinkling lights. We rolled our windows down and heard the church bells. So romantic. Much better than the time I went with Tom Brand when I was seventeen and I had to constantly fend off Mr. Octopus Hands."

Ruby's face fell. "Dallas didn't kiss you, huh?"

"Oh, there was plenty of kissing. Believe me. But it was more than that. He's kind and funny and we have this connection. I know I wanted him out of the space at first, but now I can't imagine the salon without his store in front. You should see the dividing wall he made to separate our businesses. It's stunning. I didn't even have to ask. He just did it."

"Go, Dallas," Ruby said, raising her brows. Then she busied herself toying with the display. "How does your mom feel about you two seeing each other?"

I groaned. "I haven't told her that part of it. She's trying to set me up with Tom Brand." Ruby's eyes went wide. I plunged onward. "He looks good on paper, and I really liked him in high school. But what he and I had was nothing compared to how I feel about Dallas. My mom will never understand. She saw us kiss, but I think she's blown it off as an accident or mistake or something. If she knew I'd fallen for him, it would devastate her."

Ruby laid a hand over mine. "I'm sorry, Morgan."

I knew exactly how sorry she was. She'd been there that day when Grace had fallen and died. She'd also been there when Mom had rounded on Dallas, screaming that it was his fault. That my mom had never forgiven him was no secret. That she would never forgive him was a given.

As far as my mom was concerned, Dallas was the last man in the world she wanted in her family. In her mind, he'd already cost her the one member of her family she'd loved the most. I didn't know which part of that hurt me the worst.

CHAPTER FOURTEEN

The night before our grand opening, I stood in the C.M. Salon slash Parker's Furniture store, a smile forming at what I saw. The front space held Dallas's furniture, all of it arranged in smart groupings that invited people to sit on gorgeous sofas, in carved and polished chairs, enjoy one of the magazines fanned on coffee tables, or sit down at a dining room table and chair set.

A second tree had been set up near one of the sofas and at that moment I could believe that this was a home that I wanted one day for myself. My gaze fell on the tall and wide partition screen, which was cleverly fashioned so that the front section would be hidden from view and the patrons of my salon could relax in the privacy and calm décor of the part of the business space that was mine.

Mine. All mine. Finally.

The back half, my half, had neutral walls and hardwood floors, modern mirrors and chairs, and a small even more private section that had a tiny room filled with a massage table and some potted plants, a shelf of facial cleansers and waxes and other skin care things.

The divider that Dallas had built doubled as shelves on the backside and I'd spent a few happy hours arranging all of the products that I was hoping to sell to my clients.

Dallas threaded more tinsel across the branches of our second tree. "You're smiling."

"I am." I settled a drift of trim onto a high branch and said, "I can't seem to stop."

He gave me a look, the corners of his mouth curving upward. "Last I heard being happy wasn't a bad thing."

My smile immediately faded. "What if my mom hates the place? What if she thinks I should've decorated with vibrant colors instead of neutral colors? I feel like everything is on the line for me to prove to my parents that I can be a success. If I fail, then that will show that they were right and I should've just gone to work for them at the bank."

"Where is that smile I saw a minute ago?" Dallas reached for my hand, giving it a squeeze, and swinging our hands back and forth in that way of his that I found so soothing. "Opening your own business is supposed to be fun. It's not about proving anything to your parents. Don't second-guess how you decorated. You should trust yourself one hundred percent. This is your dream and that's an awesome thing."

"You're right," I said, but my happiness was still tainted by the worry that my parents wouldn't approve. I hadn't been this happy in a long time, but old habits died hard. I picked up a string of lights he'd set on the table and smiled at them. They blinked off and on, their bright colors shimmering. No plain white lights for us. "Where should we hang these now that we've finally gotten the other tree situated where we like?" I asked.

"I thought we could hang them along the ceiling." He raised his brows, but didn't move until I nodded. "Let me grab the ladder. Turn the strands off, will you? I don't want to get electrocuted."

"Sure," I said, turning them off. I held the string of lights for him as he hung them carefully, laying them across the ceiling and using double-sided tape to hold the strands in place.

He jumped off the ladder and smiled at me. "Close your eyes."

I didn't even ask why. I squeezed my eyes shut and stood there with my heart pounding and my ears straining for every sound, so I could figure out what he was doing. Footsteps. A *click*. And then footsteps again.

"Open your eyes," he said, from beside me.

I opened them and gasped as I tipped my head back so I could check out our handiwork. The room was dark, the regular overheads cut off and the Christmas lights sparkled and danced like brilliant stars against the ceiling.

I cried out, "It's beautiful."

"Very beautiful," he said in a husky voice. But he was looking at me and not the lights. My belly did a little flip. "Wait," he said, holding up his index finger.

"Wait? For what?" I asked, but he'd already turned away and sauntered over to the music system we'd installed.

He fiddled with the remote and then soft music filled the room. Suddenly Martina McBride's voice came through the speakers singing "White Christmas." My smile grew wider and my heartbeat raced as he came toward me, a strong figure even in the dim light.

"I love this song," I admitted, shyly. "If only we really would have a white Christmas this year. I'd love that so much, but it would take a miracle for the temperature to drop in time."

"You never know," he said, holding his hand out. "May I have this dance?"

"Absolutely," I said.

He pulled me into his embrace. I felt the strength of his firm body against mine as he led me across the wooden floor with one hand on the small of my back and the other holding my hand. Together, we moved in a slow and revolving circle under the lights.

Suddenly feeling shy, I lifted my lashes. "This reminds me of prom."

"I would've liked to have taken you to prom."

My belly fluttered. "I wish you had."

"Me, too." He pulled me closer still, so close that I could feel the beat of his heart and see the steady pulse at the hollow of his throat. "You went with Tom your senior year. You wore a long white dress that had a princess skirt thing."

I burst into laughter at the apt description and he twirled me expertly. "I'll never live that down." I groaned. "I was the Prom Bride, that's what Ruby called me. In my defense, my mom picked out that dress. She said the dress I wanted was too short and too tight."

He shifted and stepped and I followed, every point of contact between us feeding the emotions welling up between us. Butterflies danced in my belly. My skin tingled and my body sagged against his to get even closer to him.

"You looked beautiful." He smiled and then winked at me. "Even when your dress knocked over that appetizer table."

We both laughed at the same time.

I leaned in and let him guide me. "You remember that?"

His chest vibrated beneath my cheek. "It's hard to forget."

I grimaced but laughed at the same time. "I think the contents of that punchbowl were still stuck in the underskirt when I got home."

Our laughter drifted along, following the strains of another Christmas song. Dancing with Dallas felt pure and sweet and real. I never wanted it to end. I let out a heavenly sigh before lifting my face to his. He gazed into my eyes. Then his mouth came down on mine.

The hushed music, the lights in the darkness, the feel of his mouth and his body, the touch of his hand—steady and sure—all combined with his woodsy scent made my knees weak. My emotions spun under the sweet power of that kiss. Every breath, every second, melded into a flawless moment, which made me forget everything but us.

We finally pulled back. He looked at me through heavy-lidded eyes. The music shifted again, this time to "Silent Night," which was my very favorite Christmas song. We kept dancing, swaying back and forth, letting our bodies touch while the music spilled over us in soft waves.

"I wish I'd been good enough for you back then. If I had been then maybe you would never have gone to prom with that toad."

I laced my fingers through his. "If we could go back in time, I'd do things differently. Or maybe that's where we are now?" I suggested.

"I like where we are now," he whispered, the corners of his mouth lifting as he tucked a piece of hair behind my ear. "How was dinner at the club?"

"I wish you'd been there. It would've been nice to have an ally. Although maybe that wouldn't have worked out so well," I said, looking down at my feet.

He lifted my chin. "Why not?"

I sighed, having trouble meeting his eyes. "My mom."

His fingers spread against my back. "She doesn't approve of me."

"Pretty much," I said, resting my head against his chest

again. The song kept going, but he paused, holding me close under the canopy of happy and beautiful lights. "I don't know what to do about her, Dallas."

"Morgan—"

"I know what you're going to say, so please don't." I shook my head, because I didn't want him to tell me again that the accident wasn't my fault. Because I knew it wasn't true.

"Morgan, I need to tell you something."

I whispered, "What is it?"

"I need to answer your question from before." His voice was low and tight, the strain perfectly audible. Suddenly, my stomach bubbled with worry. Was he about to tell me he'd run into Nina again? That he'd never gotten over her? Or that he'd met someone else.

I braced myself. "Just say it."

He dropped his forehead to mine. "You're the reason I never fell in love with anyone."

My vision blurred. "Me?"

"Nobody I dated could hold the slightest candle to you." He cupped my face in his hands and held me there, his voice shaky. "I left here because I wasn't good enough for you. I was bitter and troubled. I knew I had to become someone worthy of you."

His words made my heart feel two seconds away from exploding.

"Oh, Dallas . . ." I lifted onto my tiptoes and pressed my mouth to his.

I wanted to tell him that I loved him and that I'd always loved him. I wanted to tell him so much that it hurt. But I might have to choose between my family and him, so that kept me silent. It hit me like a ton of bricks that was exactly what was coming. But what *could* I do?

Like a million times in my life, I wished that Grace were

here. Not because her presence would change anything between my mom and me, but because I longed for my big sister. As a little girl, whenever I was sad she would hug me and assure me everything was going to be all right. But as much as I needed her, she was still gone. So I just kissed Dallas with all of the love in me, hoping I'd never have to break his heart.

CHAPTER FIFTEEN

On Monday evening, the eighteenth of December, I flipped the sign hanging on the front door—of the C.M. Salon slash Parker's Furniture—from open to closed. Our first day had been a roaring success. Just as I opened my mouth to say so to Dallas, he went to our sound system and blasted "Jingle Bell Rock" over the speakers.

I turned to praise his song choice, but he disappeared around the corner. I blinked, wondering where he'd gone. Before I could call his name, there was a knock on the front door. I swiveled, glancing at the front door to find Ruby's nose pressed against the window.

She pointed to the locked doorknob. I grinned and pointed to the closed sign. She held up a box with the logo of Jingle Bells Bakery on the sides and then flipped the lid open to reveal gloriously browned and iced cinnamon rolls nestled inside the box.

I unlocked the door and opened it. "Well played."

"Nobody can resist Jingle Bells Bakery's cinnamon rolls." Ruby swooped in, wearing a thick camel coat over a long-sleeved sweater, a tartan skirt over black leggings, and bright red suede boots with a thick treaded sole. She started dancing to the loud music, snapping her fingers as she bounced. "Congratulations on your first day!" she said.

"Thank you!" I locked the front door again and then took a deep and appreciative sniff of cinnamon, pastry, vanilla, and butter. "How did you get them this time of day and hot ones to boot? I assumed she closed early on weekdays."

"I have connections." Ruby curtsied, bowing her head. "I groom her Schnauzer, who's a complete diva. Not to mention she bites. A lot."

I inhaled the aromas coming out of the box again. "That's the real difference between doing hair on a dog versus hair on a human. Most humans don't bite."

Ruby's eyes glowed with laughter. "Only most? Not all?"

I winced. "There's a little boy in town whose objections to having his hair cut went from screaming to biting today."

Ruby exhaled a long breath. "Ouch. How'd you handle that one?"

"I solved the problem," I said, tapping my temple. "Turned out he was scared that the scissors might cut his ears. So, I made him ear protectors out of foam rollers. After that he was golden."

Ruby patted my arm. "You're going to be a great mom one day."

"Mom? Me?" My mind drifted back to that imaginary scene with Dallas and kids on Christmas Eve. My throat closed. I did want a family. A lot. I hadn't known how much until I'd come home and fallen in love. Kids had never been on my radar before.

A hard *rap-rap-rap* on the door sounded out, shattering my thoughts.

"What's Connor doing here?" I asked, unlocking the front door and turning the knob for the second time that evening.

Connor came in on a gust of cold wind. His scarf was knotted casually around his neck, his cheeks were red from the cold, and he was bearing a large bouquet of mixed flowers.

"Are those for me?" I asked, squealing.

"Nah." Connor shook his head. His coat wore a dusting of the fake snow people were spraying in their shop windows. "They're for Dallas. Think he'll like them?"

I burst into laughter. "Give me those."

"Congrats, sis." Connor shoved the flowers at me.

I turned toward the divider as Dallas came strolling out from the back with a giant smile on his face and a bottle of champagne in his hand. He stopped in his tracks, sniffing the air. "Something smells good. Is that cinnamon rolls?"

I nodded. "Jingle Bells Bakery no less. Ruby brought them. And you must have a nose like a greyhound. Let me grab a vase for these. Do you mind if I put them on that table by the tree?"

He lowered the bottle to the tabletop I'd asked about. "Not at all." Dallas gave Ruby a warm hug. Then he and Connor exchanged one of those awkward one-armed hugs guys give each other. "Good to see you, man. Let me get more glasses."

Dallas went in the back to get glasses while Ruby and Connor sat down. Ruby fussed around with napkins and a few plastic utensils, while I arranged the flowers in a pretty glass. Dallas came back and popped the cork on the bottle. The champagne flowed out and he gave a cheerful hoot as he filled the glasses and then took a seat beside me on the sofa.

"You two are the talk of the town," Ruby said. "I heard Addie Wilcox say her husband *has* to get a pedicure at the C.M. Salon. Her exact words were that he has the worst toenails ever and if she can get him in the door to look at a piece of furniture it's only a small step further to the pedicure chair."

Our laughter rang out, all four of us at the same time.

Dallas chortled. "I can't imagine a guy getting a pedicure."

Connor hit him in the arm "I get one, several times a year in fact."

Dallas's mouth fell open. "You're kidding."

I cut in. "Nope. Lots of men get pedicures. It's good for your feet."

Dallas's eyebrows lifted. His gaze moved down to his shoes as if he couldn't imagine it. "For real?"

I smiled sweetly. "And you could use a manicure as well."

His lips twisted. "Are you offering to give me one?"

I studied his face. "Are you willing to *let* me give you a manicure?"

He chuckled. "I'll let you stick with your regular clientele. Although I like the part where you'd be holding my hand."

Connor glanced from Dallas to me after that comment and then his facial expression changed as if in recognition that Dallas and I were more than just friendly business neighbors. If he had a problem with that, it didn't show.

"Your loss." I smiled at Dallas, thinking we'd find another way for me to hold his hand. I took a bite of my cinnamon roll and moaned with delight. The sweet and sticky confection clung to my tongue and throat, imparting another layer of sweetness to the day. It had been a good day, and a profitable one as well. Happiness sizzled into my being at the thought of the income earned and how much that would offset what I'd spent to get the salon up and running.

Ruby popped a piece of roll in her mouth and chewed thoughtfully. "I heard that the ladies who run the Christmas Mountain bus tours are planning on putting your beauty salon slash furniture store on their tour. Tourism is down, as you know, but your place is such a novelty. They get tourists who get tired and cranky from being on a bus all day and they claim to want to buy stuff that isn't the usual souvenir type so you might get some new business that way."

I let the champagne settle on my tongue and the delicious bubbly fizzed and popped, before I swallowed it down. "That's wonderful news, Ruby. I'll have to remember to go by their booth and thank them for thinking of us. I'll offer them a discount on some services for putting us on their route."

Connor clapped his hands. "There's your business degree kicking in, sis."

"Very funny." I lifted an eyebrow at him. "I was just genuinely being nice. How are things at the bank? Besides the new car."

"Can't complain," he said, licking crumbs off his lips before dabbing them with a napkin for good measure. "Hey, Dallas. How were furniture sales today?"

Dallas set his glass on the table. His face radiated pride. "Great. I sold an entire living room set and a kitchen table, plus a few cabinets. It was a good opening day."

"Congratulations, Dallas." Ruby lifted her champagne glass in his direction, before turning to me. "I heard you were booked solid today, Morgan."

I swallowed another bite of warm and gooey roll. "Yes! Probably because the location's so convenient."

"I don't buy that." Ruby leaned forward and her free hand touched my leg. "Location helps, but you're uber-good at what you do. Everyone knows it."

My mood immediately flat-lined. "Not everyone thinks that, actually.

Other than re-decorating the tree—which I hadn't asked her to do—my mom hadn't done one single thing to help or support me. Even my dad had loosened up enough to stop in and give me a hug and well wishes during the lunch hour, but Mom? Nope.

Ivy Reed had a backbone made of steel and no way was she about to snap herself in half to admit she might be wrong about anything, much less about my being a terrific beautician.

"Don't let Mom's issues spoil your opening day," Connor said.

"Why can't she support me, though? I mean, Emma Winters—from my choir team—called today and made an appointment for January. And Joy Evans from the choir team came by the salon today to support me and I hadn't talked to her in years."

"Joy?" Ruby asked. "I didn't know she's back in town. That's so sweet of her to drop by on your special day."

"Right?" I smiled. I shouldn't have been surprised, though. Joy was always around when we needed her, quietly lending an ear. Never judging. We'd hugged and picked things up where we left off like no time had passed. "She even made an upcoming hair appointment for both her and Carol Bennett for this Thursday. They want their hair to look fabulous for the Christmas extravaganza."

Dallas leaned forward, his elbows on his knees. "That's cool that the seven of you will perform again for Ms. King at the annual extravaganza. It's like the good ole days."

"Definitely," I agreed. "And even though I haven't talked to Joy and everyone in years, my best friends from high school showed support for my new business. But not my own mother. It really hurts."

"We support you." Dallas reached over and took my hand. I turned my head to look at him, a smile forming despite my flattened spirits. "I've never seen so many people with shampoo-commercial-worthy hair in my entire life," he said.

The compliment made my smile widen, but then it wavered. My heart ached and my mood fell again. Would my mom ever see that I was doing what I loved? That I was good at it and that I took a lot of pride in it? That it was my passion?

Probably not.

She'd somehow managed to foist Grace's youthful dreams onto my shoulders. She honestly couldn't recall that it had been Grace who had been into the bank and not me. She either wouldn't see it or didn't care to remember it that way.

Grace had loved the bank, and I was not Grace. I could never be Grace. Even I had admired my big sister, who really had seemed perfect in every way. I didn't know how to be the only daughter my mom had left, without being a huge disappointment.

"Look how sweet, Connor." Suddenly, Ruby clinked her glass into my brother's. "Dallas and Morgan are holding hands."

Connor glanced at us with a smirk. "Aww..."

I groaned. "Stop it, you two. Please."

Connor knocked back a sip of champagne. "I see my sister's stalking finally worked on you Dallas."

My mouth fell open. "I didn't stalk him," I squeaked out.

Ruby wiggled her eyebrows. "Maybe not *this* time. But when you were younger—"

"Aren't you supposed to be on my side?" I asked, gaping at her.

Ruby laughed and dusted crumbs off her sweater. "I am on your side, Morgan. That's why I said *maybe* not this time."

Dallas squeezed my hand. "I can attest to the fact that there was no stalking."

I glanced over at him. "Thank you."

He drank down the last bit of champagne in his glass. The Christmas music swirled around us, the lights on the ceiling twinkled, and the tree glowed. I wanted to be happy right now, but something was missing.

My mom was mad at me, still refusing to accept my life choices. She would probably never step a single foot into the salon, or accept Dallas and me. I hated letting those things get in the way of my being happy about the grand opening. But I loved my mom.

Dallas clapped his hands. "I have an idea. Let's go to Flat Rock."

"Where?" Ruby asked.

"You know the place." Connor elbowed Ruby in a way that made me wonder what he wasn't saying. "That big granite slab at that bend in Christmas River on the south side of town."

Ruby's cheeks heated. "Oh, right."

"I'll bring another bottle of champagne," Dallas said, seeming oblivious to their curious exchange. "Let's get moving."

I gnawed my bottom lip. "It's pretty cold out tonight."

"There's a fire ring back there," Dallas said. "I have a cord of wood in the truck. We can make a fire and drink champagne, while watching the stars. It'll be a night to remember."

My mouth stretched into a smile. "Okay, I'm in."

After the day I'd had, a night to remember sounded perfect.

CHAPTER SIXTEEN

The fire pit at Flat Rock sat next to the enormous flat rock that gave the place its name, and the view from just above the river was stunning. The water below glinted under the waning light, like a wide dark ribbon running along the banks. The occasional splash and croak and chirp of insects and other things lent a soft counterpoint to the music of the river flowing between the rocks.

The fire was up and burning, the flames glowing reddish-orange. The moon sailed above, fat and silver, and stars pricked the sky. Even though the rocks behind us blocked the wind, a chill came through the air making me shudder.

Dallas slipped his arm around me, pulling me closer to him. Much better.

Connor threw a small rock over the edge and then turned to Dallas. "You remember the time we talked Morgan and Ruby into sliding down the rocks on that old sled?"

"Definitely." Dallas chuckled, giving me a squeeze.

"That was here?" Ruby asked, laughing. "I'd totally forgotten."

"You claim that thing was a sled, bro?" I burst into laughter at the description. "It was only the bottom of a sled, remember? Someone had broken the *actual* sled and passed the remainder onto you two crazies. Then you guys talked Ruby and me into getting on that contraption."

Ruby held her champagne glass aloft, gesturing to the river. "I blame the heat for making me agree to slide on that thing. It was like a hundred and ten that day. Clearly the heat had given us a case of temporary insanity."

Connor leaned toward her. "Looks like that dunk in the river cured your being hot."

"I'd say so." Ruby gave him a mock glare. "Even in the summer, that water was freezing."

"So cold," I agreed, remembering back to that day and the memories we'd all shared.

"I can't believe you chickens agreed," Connor said, laughing.

"In our defense, you double dared us to try it." I sipped the bubbly in my glass, the delicious flavor dancing along my tongue. Then I held up my empty glass. "Who's got the bottle?"

"Right here," Dallas said, lifting the bottle and giving me a refill. "Anyone else?"

Ruby shook her head. "That was the last dare I ever took, thank you very much."

"Probably a wise choice." Connor winked at her, knocked back the rest of his drink, and then held it out for Dallas to refill.

Sitting here with Ruby, Connor, and Dallas, caused a warm feeling of comfort to roll over me. "You know what's weird?" I asked, knowing the champagne was affecting my mood and making me mushy. "I'd go to the beach in Miami and I loved the sand, surf, and sun. . . What's not to like? But I missed this river. I missed home."

"Home missed *you*," Ruby said, reaching out to squeeze my arm. "We're glad you're back."

"Definitely." Connor raised his glass, clinking it against mine.

"Can't argue with that." Dallas clinked his glass to mine and then brushed his lips against my cheek, sending tingles across my skin. Dreamy sigh.

My heart felt light and my mood had lifted. But just like *that* I remembered my mom hadn't shown up at my salon or spoken to me on the first day I'd embarked on my dream. Tears blurred my vision. I suddenly felt overwhelmed with emotion, but I didn't want to ruin everyone's happy mood. I needed a breather to compose myself.

As Dallas and Connor began discussing a funding problem with the community center where the Christmas Extravaganza would be held, I told Ruby I'd be back in a minute. I set my empty flute on the upturned log we'd been using as a table and stepped toward the river.

"Where are you going?" Dallas asked, his voice unusually concerned.

"Just taking a better look at the water." I rolled my eyes at his over-protectiveness. Although, I did find it completely adorable. My heart swooned. In my black, heeled boots I walked across the hard granite then swayed momentarily near the edge.

"Morgan, be careful." Dallas's voice rang out with a sharp edge from somewhere behind me that suddenly seemed very far away.

"Don't *worry*." I held my arms up, wanting to reassure him that I was fine and he could go back to his conversation. I turned to face him, but must've moved too fast because my foot slipped, jerking me backward. Thankfully, my arms were out so I regained my balance as I took a step backward to steady myself.

But the only thing my back foot landed on was empty space.

My arms flew up and flailed around me but there was nothing to grab onto. I opened my mouth and the words I fought to say—*no, help, this is not goo*d—turned into a short, sharp scream. The foot, hanging over into the space beyond the rocks, went down all of a sudden.

Then the rest of my body toppled sideways as well.

As I fell off Flat Rock, time felt funny. It stretched out like warm taffy. My body arced and hung in the air for an eternity and then tumbled toward the river at a gut-wrenching speed. I could see the sharp silver stars above me, the shape of the moon's face, the sides of the rocks as I went past them, and the smell of the river came to me—all mineral-laden mud and moving water.

I was falling.

All of the breath knocked out of my lungs. Even though I couldn't speak, the helpless feeling vibrating through my chest made my mind scream to *do* something to *stop* falling, but there was nothing to be done. Like it or not, I was going down.

A horrific pain lanced into my skull as I hit the water. The ice-cold river soaked through my clothes, immediately chilling me to the bone. My head immersed and I frantically kicked until I reached the surface. When my head popped out of the river, I sucked in a breath, noticing the others at the edge of the flat rock, gaping down at me.

Then the water rushed into my nose and mouth and they disappeared from sight. I coughed and sputtered, spitting out water. The cold was so complete that my body went numb. I went under again, the cold water dragging me lower this time.

Everything within me screamed to fight, to get back to the surface, but the numbing icy water held me in its grasp and wouldn't let me come up.

"It's going to be all right, sis," came a familiar female voice.

Holding my breath, I blinked. That voice—I knew that voice. I was still under water and my soaked clothes felt thick and heavy, weighing me down. My skull was in agony but that voice blanketed me in comfort.

I forced my eyes open. My lips shaped a single word that was also a question as I stared at the young girl floating before me. "Grace?"

Her blue eyes comforted me as she gave me her warm smile. "Don't worry. Everything is going to be all right."

Tears wanted to come but the water, the pain, the strangeness of seeing my sister again, held me fast as I stared at her. It was the young Grace I'd known. The big sister I'd looked up to. I'd never been so scared in my life, but at the same time I'd never been so comforted.

"I miss you," I whispered. I could feel a slow beat in my chest but it was slowing down.

"I'm always with you." Grace moved closer to me. Her hair floated around her shoulders and there was a smile on her face. I wanted to reach out and touch her, but I couldn't move anymore. "Just hold on a few more seconds, sis," she said, then the image before me vanished.

Strong arms grabbed hold of me, pulling me upward at a fast pace. I came up out of the water, sucking in the sweet feeling of air. My whole body felt limp and my eyes were wide as I stared up at the stars. My mouth opened. "Grace . . ."

"Morgan?" Dallas's voice was low and sharp. He held me tight against his chest as we moved toward shore, his legs working hard beneath us. His face was a pale oval below the light of that waxen moon, but he looked like an angel. "Morgan? Stay with me, Morgan!" he said.

I dragged my eyes away from him and looked at the shore. Connor appeared above us, holding out his arms to me. My eyes blinked open and closed. I found air and sucked it in again. Connor grasped under my arms, pulling me up to the bank.

Ruby stood beside him, with a phone to her ear. She cried out, "She's out of the river. Please hurry!"

Wrapped in my brother's arms, I shivered uncontrollably as he murmured the same words to me over and over between his sobs. "It's going to be all right, sis. It's going to be all right . . ."

I was so confused that I turned to look at the river, wondering if Grace had told him, too.

CHAPTER SEVENTEEN

I sat huddled on the narrow hospital bed, hugging my arms close to my body. The nurses had taken my wet clothes, exchanging them for a gown and robe and some weird socks that rolled up to my knees. The socks itched like they'd sewn ants into them and I scratched mercilessly. Since the socks were marginally better than suffering the stinging sensation of having my feet freeze inside my boots, I didn't complain.

At the riverbank, Dallas had wrapped his leather jacket around me for warmth and it lay over the chair beside the bed. Dallas hadn't been allowed in to see me since he wasn't family. But Connor sat in the chair next to the bed in the sterile room.

"You feeling better?" he asked.

I lifted a hand to my head and winced. "Not especially."

Connor blew out a long breath. "You scared us."

"I scared myself, too," I admitted, dropping my hand back to the sheets.

Everything in the curtained off room smelled like strong bleach and detergent and the sounds coming from the other side of the curtain weren't encouraging. I could hear someone crying from a distance and the squeak of someone's shoe against the floor, plus a whole lot of dinging from equipment and monitors.

"I'm just glad you're okay." He squeezed my hand just as his phone beeped. He pulled the cell out of his pocket and looked down at it. "It's Dad. He's on his way back to town from a business meeting in Helena. Sorry, let me call him so he doesn't panic. I'll be right back," he said, waiting until I nodded before he left the room.

I sank back against the pillows, exhausted and wanting to take a nap. Just as I started to drift off, the curtain flew back. I popped my eyes open, shocked at what I saw.

My mom stood there, gaping at me. Neither of us spoke. I couldn't speak, because Ivy Reed never—repeat *never*—left the house looking anything less than pressed. So I'd been shocked into silence. My mom looked rumpled, to say the least. Her makeup was already off for the night and her hair, always so carefully coiffed, was in a low knot at the back of her neck. She wore a big sweater and coat and her shoes didn't match.

And it wasn't like she had on one bone-colored shoe and one taupe-colored shoe, either. On one foot she wore an ankle boot in solid black leather. On the other she had on what looked suspiciously like one of her rubber garden boots.

She stood there, her face so pale I could see the fine tracings of blue veins in her temples and her hand lifted to her mouth. She lowered that hand and then rushed the rest of the way into the room. "Morgan, are you all right? Where's the doctor? Have you had an X-ray? An MRI? Tests to make sure you're fine? That you aren't dying? Or—"

"I'm fine," I said, cutting her off so she'd stop pelting me with questions.

Her eyes widened and she turned to the door, hollering, "Someone get Dr. Blake on the phone. I want her in my daughter's room *now!*" She turned back to face me. She advanced and then took a few steps back toward the open space beyond the curtain. Her mouth worked and my heart went tight and stuttering. "I-I was getting ready to lie down. I'd put my nighttime snack by the bed and was opening my book when Cora's daughter Maggie called because her boyfriend's brother works with a guy who moonlights as a paramedic. You remember him, I'm sure. He went to school with you."

I blinked, having no idea who she was talking about. "Okay..."

Mom nodded briskly. "Well, he heard... and then he told... So, anyway. You..." She stuttered and stopped, finally walking over to the bed. Her eyes widened and then she swallowed with an audible click. "Are you okay, sweetheart? I mean, really...?"

Guilt slammed into me so hard it hurt worse than my aching head. I'd scared my poor mom. She'd already buried one daughter and now I'd freaked her out again.

"I'm fine, Mom. Don't worry," I said.

She twisted her fingers together and then began straightening the sheets and covers, aligning the edges until they were perfectly straight. Then her gaze met mine. "What were you thinking going up to Flat Rock so late this time of year?"

"We were celebrating," I said, surprised that she'd gone from concerned to scolding me so quickly. "The river looked so pretty and I stepped closer to get a better look and..." And I'd had too much champagne and wasn't paying attention to how close I was to the edge. Stupid, stupid, stupid me. I looked away. "I didn't mean to worry you."

"Well, you did." Mom's cry cracked my heart. "I-I thought..."

"I'm sorry," I said, knowing what she'd thought. I tried to reach for her but she turned away, her hands going to her face.

When she spoke again her voice was muffled and hoarse. "What were you thinking? Why were you even out there? Flat Rock's dangerous in the daylight. They should rope that place off, all those rocks get wet and cause people to slip and fall."

"I'm sorry," I repeated, swallowing back hurt that had nothing to do with my injuries. I understood what she was going through and I'd caused that hurt and worry after everything she'd already been through with Grace. "It was an accident."

She turned to face me. The tip of her nose was red. "You shouldn't have been there in the first place. What on earth would possess you to go out there at night?"

"We'd had such a good day, so Dallas suggested—"

"Dallas Parker." Mom's voice held anger and agony. "Of course it had been his suggestion. He's always been reckless and he still is. Why can't you see he's going to hurt you? You need someone who's never going to put you in harm's way."

My eyes overflowed with tears. "We're good together, Mom. Everyone's talking about our businesses—"

"A furniture store and a beauty salon?" She shook her head, blowing out a breath. "That makes no sense. You belong in the bank with your family," she said, slipping onto the bed next to me, encircling me with her arm.

Completely exhausted, I rested my face against her neck, which smelled like the lily-scented cream she used at night—a scent I'd known since I was little. "I'm twenty-six years old, Mom. I love my salon and what I do. I don't *want* to work at the bank. I wouldn't enjoy it. Why can't you believe that?"

There were no answers from her and I'd known that there wouldn't be. Tears ran down my cheeks and I cried, wanting nothing more than to hug her and to have her hug me back and for everything to be okay between us. It couldn't be, though. Not while my heart was away from the bank and in my salon and with Dallas.

"Can't you try working at the bank, sweetheart?" Mom sniffed beside me, tears streaming down her face. "It would mean so much to me to have you close. Away from whatever Dallas Parker would suggest next that would get you hurt."

I sighed. The feel of her arms around me made me feel safe and I was scared in so many ways. I couldn't argue Dallas had a history of being around accidents. He wouldn't hurt me though. Well, not unless he had rushed into things too soon with me. Or decided I wasn't enough for him, like he had with his last girlfriend. That would hurt big time.

I sighed, so terribly exhausted. "Mom . . ."

She moved back, holding my face in her hands. "It would be better for you to be with Dad and Connor, sweetheart. You can sell off your half of the shop to Dallas or something. The rest of your trust will be enough for you to move on from this little dream of yours."

Little dream. It wasn't a *little* dream. It was the whole enchilada.

And I'd made my dream come true.

My heart let out a low and painful throb that sent pain echoing through my skull. The headache clouded everything and so did fear. Would Dallas hurt me? Would I tell him I loved him only to have him break my heart?

"Will you at least think about it, sweetheart?" she asked.

"Okay, Mom." I sank against her, my eyes drifting closed as my body shut down for the night. "I'll think about it."

CHAPTER EIGHTEEN

Once the hospital released me later that night, my mom dropped me off at Ruby's where I found a note that my friend had been called to work because her manager had another "doggie emergency." I had a lot to think about and felt cooped up inside.

Even though it was late, I drove downtown and parked near the Falls. I hiked up the steps and then sat on Kissing Bench across from The Sharing Tree. My gaze fastened on the tree, trying to appreciate its beauty, but my heart felt heavy like a cement brick in my chest.

The wind had picked up and gotten harsh. It was late and dark and lonely out there but I stayed right where I was, unable to move a single inch. Everything I'd ever dreamed of had been mine for a little while. It hurt to lose it all but I didn't know what else to do. I couldn't keep having the same argument with my mom and I couldn't let her down.

It turned out that coming home had been the worst decision ever. I'd made a massive mess of my life. I should've stayed in Miami, opened the salon there. Or come home and worked at the bank and kept my feelings closed to Dallas. My heart cracked a little at the mere thought.

I'd plowed headlong into the life I wanted and where had that gotten me? I'd been reckless this evening up on Flat Rock. I'd hurt my family and the guilt was eating at me.

A black truck pulled up to a parking space below. My mouth went dry and my heart sped up. I looked down at my feet, not knowing if I should run to him or run from him.

Dallas hurried up the steps. "I hoped to find you here."

"Hey," I said, feeling miserable as he approached. I didn't want to hurt him. But whatever decision I made was going to hurt someone.

He took a seat beside me. "I called you a dozen times but didn't hear back. I went to Ruby's and she said you left a note that you'd gone for a walk."

I swallowed and lifted my eyes to the sky, which was dark and studded with glittering stars that shined like the dreams I once had. "Yeah, I needed to get out."

"I heard you're closing your side of the shop."

"Not necessarily." My lips were numb from cold and misery. But it didn't surprise me how fast Ivy Reed could spread news, even though I'd yet to make a decision.

"Why would you even think of doing that?" He reached for my hand but I stuffed my hands into the pockets of my coat.

"I told my mom I'd think about working at the bank. That's all," I said.

"But you would hate that." His voice was gentle, his fingers tugging gently at my chin so I'd face him. My head turned but I kept my eyes down. "What's this about, Morgan?"

I bit my lip. "It's about me needing my mom in my life and not having her upset with me all the time. She's afraid you'll do something to hurt me and . . . you might. You like taking risks and you talk everyone into doing those things with you,"

I said, reiterating my mom's words that were circling in my head.

He frowned, a line forming between his eyebrows. "I'm not that guy anymore."

"At least you admit you used to cause trouble," I said, my gaze flicking to Kissing Bench and triggering the memory of that time Tom and I had been here making out by the Falls. "Why did you hit Tom?"

"Just let that go, Morgan."

"No," I said, wanting to know what prompted him to do that. "Tom dumped me after you punched him. I want to know why you did that. Did seeing us together make you jealous?"

"Yes, but that's not why I hit him." He raked a hand through his short, dark hair and blew out a breath. Then he turned to me. "I'd caught him kissing another girl earlier that day. When I saw him there with you . . . I lost it."

I blinked. "He cheated on me?"

"Yes." He seemed to take no pleasure in letting me know.

"What a tool." I shook my head, glad that he'd dumped me and I hadn't wasted more time on him. "You can't just go around hitting people, though. And that's not the only stunt you pulled."

He leaned forward with his elbows on his knees before giving me a side-glance. "Want to know why I used to do all those things?"

Tears misted my vision. "Yes."

"I was a scared kid who nobody seemed to care about one way or the other. I wanted attention. Given my situation at home, I craved it. So I got it in any way I could. It was stupid and immature and dangerous. I know that. But I'm not that guy anymore."

"What changed?" I asked.

He paused, blowing out a breath. "After graduation, we went back to the classrooms to get our diplomas. After I got mine, your choir teacher, Ms. King pulled me aside."

A chill vibrated through me. "She did?"

He nodded. "I remember her words like it was yesterday. She said, '*I see a fire burning in your eyes, Dallas. Like life gave you a bad hand and you're angry about that, so you're going to prove to everyone that you're as bad as they say.*"

More chills vibrated up and down my spine as he paused. "Go on . . ."

He sucked in a breath. "She went on saying, '*A lot of people don't expect much from a kid that comes from a difficult home. But you can't let people's low expectations keep you from achieving your dreams. What's important to you, dear boy? What do you love? Figure it out and go after it. Because nobody can stop you if you believe in yourself. Remember that.*"

A hot tear rolled down my cheek as I stared at him, the moonlight outlining the angles of his handsome face. His brown eyes were in shadows, but I could still see the strength in them. I swiped at the tears spilling down under my chin. "I'm glad you found your strength."

He nodded. "What about yours?"

I waved my hands. "Just let me be. Please."

He shook his head. "I can't do that."

"Why not?" I stood, and started backing away. "Why can't you let me go?"

He stood, moving in front of me. "Because I love you."

I lifted my lashes and met those warm brown eyes, open and vulnerable in front of me. My heart squeezed, but I was overwhelmed. I wanted to curl up against him, breathe in that smell of lumber that was all him, and feel the strength of his arms around me. I wanted to believe that we could last, that together we were stronger than anything and everything and that he would never hurt me. But my emotions swirled and I didn't know what to believe.

He tucked a piece of hair behind my ear. "I can't let you walk away from me and what we have together. I know you feel like you have to choose between your family and me. I'd never ask you to do that."

"I know you wouldn't," I said, a low sob breaking from my throat. I wanted to tell Dallas that I loved him, too. That I loved him with my very soul, which felt broken and raw. I couldn't tell him right now, though. If I did, I might cave and that would hurt my mom and I was so confused. Part of me knew that my mom was forcing me to choose between him and my family. But my emotions warred through me and I couldn't make a choice.

My mom was scared of Dallas and his uncanny ability to spread tragedy whether he meant to or not. I knew why she was scared and I knew I wasn't Grace. The horrible accident hadn't been Dallas's fault, but mine. The accident at the river was also my fault. Maybe I was the one who spread tragedy in their wake. Or maybe we were both somehow cursed.

"Whatever you decide about us, please don't sell your salon," he said, his voice firm. "Don't give up on your dreams, Morgan."

"I need my mom in my life," I protested, wishing he'd understand the torment I felt inside. "She's made it clear she'll never accept my salon. Or my relationship with you."

He shook his head. "Promise me you won't go all Stepford daughter on me again. That you won't let her destroy your life."

"It's *my* choice," I snapped, feeling pressured under the weight of his words. My face went hot. I took a step back, intending to flee but he reached for my hands, holding me in place.

"No, it's *her* choice," he said, his brown eyes piercing mine. "I know you, Morgan. You don't want the bank and that life. I know you love your business with a passion that most people never get to expend in a career. Don't give that up."

I didn't want to give that up, but I had no choice. It was that or my mom. She hadn't said it in those exact words, but she kept pushing and she always would. Because she just wanted me where she knew I was safe in her care. Feeling guiltier and more confused than ever, I stepped back and Dallas didn't try to hold onto me. He let me go.

I breathed in and out, sending white frosty plumes of my breath across the short distance between us. "Maybe I belong at the bank. I don't know."

Dallas blew out a breath. "You belong in that bank as much as I do. Don't lie to yourself, and please don't lie to me."

"I'm not lying," I said, grinding my teeth together. My insides turned hot and electric. "I'm reconsidering, that's all. I have the right to change my mind."

He reached for me. "You're not thinking straight."

"Stop pushing me!" I yelled, because his words were pushing me to make a decision—the same decision my heart wanted me to make, but my mind was in chaos right now. I took another step back from him. "I need a break from you. From us."

He flinched. "You can't mean that."

"I do," I said, nodding. My head spun and my chest felt hollow. I was drowning in a sea of stress and emotion. I had to get out of there, so I turned to walk away.

"You're leaving me?" His voice came after me on a small gust of wind, raw and filled with heartbreaking emotion.

My head dropped low. I didn't want us to be over, but I needed space. It killed me to think I might be causing him pain, that he might feel abandoned the way his mom had left him, but I was in survival mode. I needed space to decide what was right for me. Even if that meant that letting my salon go and working at the bank was the best thing.

"We need time apart." My voice was ragged as a gust of wind blew, swaying me on my feet.

He came toward me, slipping his arms around my waist. "You can't give up on us."

His words pelted me. My vision blurred and I pressed my hands to my temples, stepping out of his arms. "You're still pushing me. My mom says I won't be safe with you."

"I would never hurt you," he said, firmly.

"You already have," I said. Then I turned and started walking away, wanting my space, wanting time to *think*.

I loved Dallas. But love doesn't mean being safe. It meant being willing to risk getting hurt and I couldn't risk that right now on top of everything else. I had to think about my family and how much what I do impacts them.

As much as I needed space, part of me hoped he would come after me and tell me again that he loved me. Another part of me hoped that he wouldn't come after me, because if he said he loved me one more time, I might break down and tell him how much I loved him, too. Either way, he didn't come after me, which I told myself was a good thing. I needed to make a decision on my own, even though I felt like I'd just lost everything.

CHAPTER NINETEEN

The next day passed in a blur with Dallas and I keeping busy without speaking to each other. I'd given him back the leather jacket he'd loaned me in a very awkward exchange.

I wasn't any closer to a decision on working at the bank, either.

On Wednesday morning, I started crying after seeing the empty box of Jingle Bells Bakery's cinnamon rolls in the dumpster and knew it was time to get some advice. So, I called the one woman who had always been there for me.

Ms. King opened her bright blue front door with a smile, but she wore a tired expression and new lines were etched around her nose and lips. My heart sank with worry as I handed her the gift of beauty supplies I'd wrapped for her.

She held the door open wider. "So good to see you, Morgan. Come in."

"I brought you something to go under the tree," I said.

She reached out, her swollen fingers brushing mine and worry ate at my heart. She was one of the reasons I'd come home, one of the reasons I wanted to be home, and she'd soon be leaving us. I would appreciate every minute with her before that time came.

She took the gift, pleasure lighting her eyes. "That's thoughtful of you."

I stepped into her house and followed her into the living room. She set the present below the twinkling Christmas tree. "Would you like some hot tea? I just set the kettle."

I surveyed her weary face. "I can get it. The kettle's on you said?"

She nodded and bustled past me. "I'm not so ill that I can't serve a guest in my house. Sit and I'll bring a cup to you."

I took a seat as instructed and stared at the Christmas tree. Even though it had been less than two weeks, it felt like a lifetime had passed between the day I'd brought that tree here and now. Ms. King came back in, carrying an exquisitely arranged tray that she set down on the coffee table.

She took a seat, patting her silver hair back into place and smoothing invisible wrinkles from her silk blouse and long skirt before she said, "I heard about your accident. Are you okay?"

I sighed. "Yes, I'm fine. Let me pour please."

I took the cozy-wrapped teapot and filled a cup two-thirds of the way full before passing it to her. I poured myself a cup as well, doctoring it with cream and sugar.

Ms. King was far from ordinary or predictable. That was one of the things that drew others to her. She did things her own way and always had. Even tea. I'll admit, though, that the first time she'd set to making hot tea I'd been pretty sure she was ruining perfectly good tea and I'd been reluctant to drink it. Later, I'd been pleasantly surprised to find that I liked tea various ways. She'd always been a teacher and mentor for me. I needed her advice now more than ever.

I lifted the cup to my lips and let a swallow of the steaming, sweet and milky liquid flow into my mouth and throat. "My mom has been more controlling than ever since the accident. I'm to blame for falling into the river Monday night. I should've been paying more attention that close to the edge." I sighed. "My mom blames Dallas, though. As always."

Ms. King picked up a plate that held sugar wafers and held it out until I took one. Then she set the plate down. "I'm sure your mom is just upset that she couldn't protect you."

"You really think so?" Tears blurred my vision. "I feel like I can't live up to her expectations. She doesn't see me as anyone, but the daughter who isn't Grace."

Ms. King shook her head. "You're interpreting her actions wrong."

My mouth fell open. "I'm not wrong, Ms. King. I fell into the river and all she could talk about was Grace and how she wanted to work at their bank, so I should want to work at the bank. She wants me to be the daughter she loved most."

Ms. King sipped her tea. Her eyes studied me over the rim of her cup and when she put it down she leaned forward. "Is that what you really think, Morgan? Your dear mother lost a child from a terrible accident. For the rest of your life, she'll be afraid to lose you, too. That's the control you're feeling, her attempts to protect you."

I lowered my gaze. "You don't understand, Ms. King..."

"Hear me out." Ms. King's gentle hand rested on my arm. "What's happening right now? You opened your own beauty salon. You're also dating Dallas—and yes I heard about that. Both of these things are proof that you're slipping away from her."

I stared at her, numbly. "Go on."

"You're not a mother yet, so you don't know what it feels like to lose a child, and you don't have to have a child die to lose one. They leave and grow up, because that's what they're supposed to do. They make their own decisions and live their own lives, leaving their parents' control. She doesn't want to lose you."

I watched her sit back and bite into her cookie. Her gaze didn't waver. I mulled over what she had said. Could that be the whole crux of it? Was my mom trying to control me because she's afraid of losing me?

I looked up. "I don't know how to make her stop comparing me to Grace."

"She'll do what she'll do, but you don't have to react to it." Ms. King picked her cup up again. Her slender fingers were pale as she brought the rim to her lips and took a sip. "You just be yourself, Morgan. Your mom will adjust."

I nibbled on the cookie, which was sweet and crisp. "What if she doesn't?"

"Then that's her issue." Ms. King stood and came to sit beside me on the sofa. Her arms went around me and I leaned into that embrace. "Morgan you have to live your life and live it for you. It's not enough to wake up in the morning and go about your day, living for someone else. You have to do what's in your heart. We all do."

My eyes watered. "I don't know."

She gave my shoulder a squeeze before letting go. "Would you be happy if you did exactly what your mom wants and went to work at the bank?"

I wiped my eyes. "No."

"Then why do it?" she asked, pulling out a lace handkerchief and handing it to me. "Your mom lost her daughter. You lost a sister. But nobody is trying to live their life to make up for your pain, are they? Nobody can ease your loss, just like you can't ease your mother's loss. No matter how hard you might try. Your mom is living her life the way she wants to, right?"

My mom loved her life. She was happy in it. Everything she did was because it made her happy. I wanted to do the very same thing. I hadn't been living my life for me. I'd spent the better part of my twenties doing exactly what Ms. King had said, living my life to try to make up for my mom's loss. I'd neatly stacked my days the way she wanted, but I hadn't been living the life I wanted. I hadn't been truly happy.

I'd finally figured out what made me feel alive: My relationship with Dallas. Running my beauty salon. Being home in Christmas Mountain again.

All of these things made me truly happy. I'd felt more alive these past few weeks than I had in the past twenty years. I didn't want to lose that feeling. And the only one who could ensure I wouldn't lose the life I'd chosen was me.

CHAPTER TWENTY

Later that night, my brother picked me up for dinner at the country club with my parents. The last thing I wanted to do was have dinner at the club again, but I knew my mom was telling the whole town I was coming to work at the bank. Clients had walked into the salon today asking me how much longer I'd be open and I had to reassure them I wasn't closing down.

I couldn't avoid my mom any longer.

Connor and I walked through the festive lobby and the hostess, Elizabeth, greeted us. "Good evening, Connor, Morgan." She nodded at each of us. "Your parents are already seated. I'll take you to their table."

"Thank you," Connor and I said, in unison.

I wore a knee-skimming black frock and a colorful cashmere shawl, small hoop earrings, and a dash of makeup. I'd left my hair long and flowing, curled at the ends. Not exactly dressed up for battle, but dressed for myself in any case.

"How was your day?" Connor asked, as we walked through the dining room.

"Interesting," I said, raising my eyebrows at him. "When I

picked up my latte at Sleigh Café this morning, I ran into Brandon Wallace, who was neighbors with Faith Sterling. You know, one of my best friends from the choir team?"

"I remember Faith from the Christmas extravaganza," he said.

I nodded. "I'd heard Faith was back in town, so I asked Brandon if he'd seen her and he got this shy smile on his face when he said yes. I wonder what's going on there. Anyway, Brandon mentioned the community center is in trouble and needs funding to save it. I told him I'd do an online auction offering services from the C.M. Salon to raise money."

"I'll make sure Reed Bank contributes as well," he said.

"That's sweet of you," I said, knowing my brother had a heart of gold. Grace would've been proud of the man her little brother had become. I'd felt her presence in my heart ever since my fall into the river. I hoped Grace would be proud of me, too, especially knowing what I had to do tonight. I glanced at my brother, thinking about his offer. "I've seen Ms. King twice since I've been back and can't believe she didn't tell me about the community center's troubles when she had to know I'd be willing to help."

"Maybe she thought you had enough on your plate and she didn't want you to stress further."

"That would be so like her to do that. Sometimes I feel like she's a second mother to me," I said, grateful to have that remarkable woman in my life.

When we arrived at the table, my parents were ordering a bottle of Chardonnay from Nina. A frisson of both pain and jealousy ate at my heart when I saw her. I knew she and Dallas had dated many years ago, but I couldn't help thinking that perhaps he would date her again now that I'd so stupidly demanded I needed space from him.

Mom stood and hugged me. "You look like you're feeling better," she said.

"I feel totally fine, Mom," I said, flicking a glance at Nina.

Connor nudged my elbow. "They say cold water's great for the skin, right?"

"That's not funny," Mom snapped, even though she rarely scolded her golden boy.

Dad stood and hugged me. "Your mother says you're coming home to work at the bank. I'll talk to human resources tomorrow about clearing out an office for you."

An office. At. The. Bank.

I opened my mouth to correct him that I'd only promised mom I'd think about it—

"Hello again, Morgan." Nina gave me a brilliant smile, gesturing to the scarf wrapped around my neck. "That scarf is everything."

"Thank you." I looked down at my scarf, which was a mix of bright emerald and soft blues. I still wanted to correct my dad about the bank, but I didn't want to be rude to Nina who had always been sweet to me. It wasn't her fault I was paranoid that she might snatch Dallas up now that I'd alienated him. "I love your hairstyle, Nina," I said.

"Thanks." She smiled, patting her elegant twist. "I hear you're amazing with hair and I'm looking forward to visiting the C.M. Salon the first chance I get."

Mom bolted upright. "I'm afraid Morgan won't—"

"Could I trouble you for some tea?" I asked, interrupting my mom before she entirely ruined my business. "In addition to a glass of wine, of course," I said, hoping she'd bring more than one of the bottles my parents had ordered.

"Right away." Nina nodded and then dashed off.

I sat down, lifting the white linen napkin from the china holder and placing it on my lap. My nerves jangled as I did, my head starting to ache all over again. I'd cried so much these past two days that my eyes felt grainy and puffy.

I wanted my salon. I didn't want the bank. And I needed to tell my parents right now.

"Sorry to interrupt," Nina said, returning to the table, with an awkward gesture behind her. "But he says he's joining you?"

A sour taste filled my mouth as I spotted Tom Brand standing beside our table in all of his Nordic blondness. He looked older, but also as handsome as ever, just as fit, and well dressed in a gray pinstriped jacket and slacks. His wore a blue shirt and a striped tie.

"Good to see everyone," Tom said, giving me the biggest smile of all. "I'm glad to join you this evening. Thanks for inviting me, Mrs. Reed."

My mom had invited Tom Brand to our "family" dinner?

My jaw tightened as my gaze shot to my mom, who looked unruffled by this turn of events. She had totally set us up. Plus, she knew I had feelings for Dallas. How could she set me up with Tom? The guy was a cheater and a liar. Not that Mom knew that, I supposed.

My dad gave Tom a firm handshake and Connor muttered something unintelligible as I lifted my hand in a polite wave.

Tom gave me what I could only describe as a *suave* smile and took the seat next to me, his leg pressing against mine. Ick. I moved my leg away immediately. He placed his napkin in his lap, leaning closer to me and I refrained from the urge to slap a hand over my nose. The guy wore way too much cologne.

Not to mention that nothing compared to the scent of lumber these days.

Suddenly, Connor whipped his phone out and I wondered if he was about to take a picture of us. That would cap off my evening. A photo of me and the cheating jerk, who wore too much cologne, my shame forever captured. Oh, joy.

Mom cleared her throat. "Connor, we have a rule about no phones at the dinner table."

"Sorry, this is important." Connor's fingers flew over the screen and then he tucked the phone back inside his jacket pocket. "It was a life or death situation. Won't happen again."

I gave my brother an odd look, since he was usually the star and not the one being scolded.

"You look amazing, Morgan." Tom turned to me, looking me up and down in a way that made me annoyed. "I can't believe it's been such a long time since we've seen each other."

I gave him my sternest look and my sweetest smile. "It has been a long time. I think the last time we saw each other was at the Falls, right before graduation."

He had the good grace to color.

"You're wrong, sweetheart." Mom chimed in, obviously in the dark that I'd been referencing the time Dallas had decked my ex. "Tom was at graduation. I distinctly recall him being there. You were so close to valedictorian, too. Weren't you, Tom? Morgan's grades were close as well. Both of you have excelled academically."

"Thank you, Mrs. Reed." He nodded and lifted the wineglass Nina had just filled. Then he glanced at me before looking at my mom and dad. "I believe in hard work and would value that in a wife, even with her staying home to raise the kids."

I choked on my sip of wine at the same time Connor let out a loud cough. Was he implying I might be his future wife? At home with his kids? He had to be talking about some other woman.

Tom's hand settled on my knee, giving it a squeeze.

Oh, great. Either he didn't have another woman in mind or

he still didn't believe in monogamy. Whichever the truth, *ick*. I dropped my hand to his, promptly removing it from my knee as I flared my eyes at him.

Mom nodded as if she approved of his statement. Then she turned to me. "Morgan, did you know that Tom is a hedge fund manager in Bozeman? He travels to New York City for work. Isn't that impressive?"

"Just grand," I said, wondering if she'd be as impressed by his uninvited knee grabbing. I knocked back my drink, wondering if I should out him. No, Connor would likely bop him one. The thought momentarily perked me up. "Personally, I'd never leave Christmas Mountain again. I've grown up a lot since graduation and if I could go back in time I wouldn't make the same choices as when I was young," I gave Tom a meaningful look.

Dad's gaze moved to Tom. "So, Bozeman. . . That's not far from us, is it? Just a few hours by car if my mental calculations are correct."

"Yes." Tom laid his menu on the table. "And I work from home a lot." He gave me another smile, one so wide I could see the fillings winking in his back molars. "It seems I have more reasons to come back now."

My stomach clenched and it was a miracle I didn't toss my cookies.

Connor cut in. "Hey, Morgan. I'm thinking about calling Dallas to see if he wants to hang out later. Why don't you and Ruby tag along?"

Mom shook her head. "Morgan doesn't need to be around that man. He's reckless and—"

"The accident at Flat Rock was my fault," I snapped, finally having enough. "You can't blame Dallas because I had the lame idea to walk along the rocks in the dark. That was my decision. I'm the one who slipped and there's nobody to blame but me."

It was true. I'd done that, not Dallas and I knew that if I didn't speak in his defense my fall would have become one more rumor for the mill about how dangerous and wild he was, rumors that had already cost him in this town.

Dad cleared his throat. "The truffle-and-sweet-pea risotto looks good. So does the steak. Has anyone tried that together?"

Dead silence.

My fists balled on the table and I stared at them, trying to compose myself. My gaze wandered to the fresh manicure I'd given myself earlier, making me think about how hard I'd worked to be able to hang that sign outside my salon to do what I loved the most in the world.

"Morgan will not be seeing Dallas again," Mom said, looking so stiff even her hair seemed rigid. Her fingers showed white at the knuckles as she clutched the menu. "She's closing the salon, so they won't be sharing the space anymore either. Thank goodness."

I couldn't do it anymore. I couldn't sit there and let my mom extol the virtues of the lying cretin next to me. Ms. King had suggested that I follow my heart and live while I could and it was high time I started now.

"I'm going to see Dallas again the first chance I get after this dinner." The words came from my mouth so loudly, my mom dropped her menu. It fanned open on the tabletop. Connor's eyebrows went up and a smile played on his mouth. Dad fidgeted, his hand yanking at his tie as he looked from me to Mom. I'd never spoken to my mom that way.

"Morgan," she said, firmly.

"No." I held a hand up to halt whatever else might come from her mouth. "This is *my* life and I get to live it the way I want. I'm not Grace and I never will be. You need to stop pretending that if you make me into her then it will be like you never lost your favorite daughter."

Mom gasped. "How can you say such a thing?"

"Why else would you keep trying to make me into her?" I asked, tears welling in my eyes as my throat tightened. I knew I was making a scene, but I didn't care. It was time to tell my mom the truth, even if she hated me for the rest of my life. "Grace's accident that day at the Falls was *my* fault."

Connor reached for me. "Morgan—"

"No!" My throat tightened as all the guilt I'd been holding in since that day came to the surface and I needed to get it out. "She needs to know the truth."

Mom made a mewing sound and Dad's arm slipped around her shoulder. Connor stared at me like he wanted to say more, but I shook my head. Tom stared at the surrounding restaurant, probably because people were starting to stare. But I didn't care about being the good girl anymore. I would never be the perfect daughter and I was exhausted from trying.

"We'd *all* wanted to go on that nature walk that day. But I was dancing around and not paying attention to where I was going. I slipped . . ." My voice trailed off as a sob escaped at the admission. "And I'd started to fall off the cliff, but Grace reached out and grabbed me. She pulled me to safety and she fell instead. Your favorite child died because of me."

I hated that I was hurting her. But I had no other choice. I had to let go of the past. I couldn't live with the guilt any longer, even if I lost my mom in the process.

"Morgan," Mom said, her face going white.

"I should've told you I'd slipped," I said, sniffling, knowing I'd lost my mom for good. She'd never forgive me for the mistake that had cost us our family, but I had to learn to forgive myself. "I kept that secret to myself all of these years. I knew you'd hate me if you found out that I slipped and—"

"I already knew," she said, quietly. "And I love my children equally. You. And Connor. And Grace, may she rest in peace. You're all a part of me. You should never be afraid to tell me anything. I'm your mother."

I flinched. "H-How did you know?"

"I told her," Connor said, his green eyes welling. "I saw you slip, sis. I had no idea you'd been keeping that in. I've *never* blamed you for Grace's fall, either. She saved you because she loved you. If I could've reached you in time then it would've been me who'd fallen."

My mom gasped and I realized tears were falling down her perfectly made-up face. My dad pulled her closer to him as he rubbed her shoulder lovingly.

"You're right," I said, the thought of losing Connor making me sick to my stomach. "If I'd seen Grace or you falling, I would've done anything to save you both, too. I never knew you'd seen me slip and I've felt guilty all this time."

"I never blamed you for Grace's death, Morgan," Mom said, her tone firm.

"No." I shook my head. "You've blamed Dallas all of this time. He suggested we go on that nature walk, but we all wanted to go. Even Grace. It wasn't his fault."

"I know," she said, shocking me. She brought her hand to her chest and bit her bottom lip, a habit that was usually mine. "I shouldn't have blamed Dallas when I'm the one who left you kids alone that day. If anyone is to blame, it's me."

"Ivy . . .?" Dad asked, his voice broken with shock. "I will not have any of that talk from you or Morgan. Am I at fault for being at work that day? For not protecting my daughter as a father should?" His tone made it obvious he'd weighed that guilt himself. "Grace's fall was a terrible accident. Nobody is to blame. I've let you blame Dallas, Ivy, and I probably should've put a stop to it. But you were grieving and no family should have to suffer this loss."

I stared at my mom, who looked back at me through red eyes. "I've been trying to make up for Grace's death by being who you want me to be, Mom. And I'm miserable. Is that what you want for me?"

"No . . ." She reached across the table, but her fingers stopped just short of touching mine. "I want you to be happy. That's all I've ever wanted. You seem to be floundering. I want to help you get back on course."

"We all want that." Tom's hand came down on my knee again.

"You really need to stop, Tom." My teeth clenched as I shoved his hand away. "I'm not off course, Mom. I've returned to Christmas Mountain and am doing what makes me happy."

Tom knocked back a sip of wine and then set the glass down. "Morgan, surely you must know that opening a beauty salon is hardly the most financially beneficial way to spend the money your grandparents left you. I could help you with some lucrative investments."

I looked at Tom, who smiled in return, making my stomach roil.

"Do you think I don't know you cheated on me when we were together?" I asked, gesturing to Tom. "That's right, everyone. This golden boy dumped me because Dallas caught him cheating on me and then socked him one."

Tom choked on his drink.

"Oh, my goodness." Mom's eyes went wide and she placed a hand to her chest.

Dad's eyes narrowed as he slapped his menu onto the table with a loud *thump*. "You did *what* to my daughter?" he demanded.

"Um . . ." Tom squirmed in his seat, reaching up to loosen

his tie. Probably trying to figure out a way to weasel out of this situation. Ha!

"Dallas!" Connor called out, waving his hand in the direction behind me. "About time you got here, man. Glad you got my text. Care to join us?"

CHAPTER TWENTY-ONE

My heart leapt at the sight of Dallas. His dark-brown hair was mussed, there was sawdust on the tee shirt he wore under his leather jacket, and the knees of his jeans had stiff shiny patches that told me he'd been working with varnish and sealant when he'd received Connor's text.

Nina had apparently escorted Dallas to our corner and she backed away nonchalantly, serving a nearby table. We'd gathered a bit of an audience at first, but people were politely pretending *not* to stare at the moment.

I was so shocked to see Dallas here that I couldn't think for a second and when I could think I wondered if I were dreaming the entire thing. In his work attire, he looked so out of place here at the country club and yet so utterly perfect at the same time.

The red-haired hostess, Elizabeth, dashed up, clearly flustered. She squeaked out, "Sir, you need a dinner jacket to be here. We have a few in the back and—"

"No, thank you, ma'am," he said, nodding to her. "I'm not here for dinner. I'm here for *her*. A jacket isn't necessary for what I'm about to do."

My mouth dropped open. Was he going to haul me out over his shoulder, alpha-male style?

Yes, please.

My brain cleared after I blinked a few times. I watched Dallas stand there, looking from me to my folks and his gaze flicked briefly to Tom, his expression impassive.

Connor grinned and sat back, his eyebrows lifting slightly.

Dallas took a deep breath. "Morgan, I'm sorry to interrupt. But I need to talk with you."

Tears filled my eyes. "Okay . . ."

The hostess clapped her hands together in prayer position. "But, sir. Wearing a dinner jacket is one of our rules."

I choked on a mixture of laughter and sobs. "Dallas has never cared much for rules."

"I think we have one in your size, sir," she said, wringing her hands together, before she sped off.

"Wine?" Connor lifted a glass in Dallas's direction, but Dallas shook his head. Connor guffawed, before bringing the glass to his own mouth. "Hope nobody minds if I indulge."

"What are you doing here, Dallas?" Mom asked, her cold tone slightly confused.

"I'm sorry to barge in on your dinner like this, Mr. and Mrs. Reed." Dallas raised his palms, his tone apologetic, but firm. "I know you blame me for a lot of things and I get it. I was young and stupid and reckless. I did a lot of things in the past that put your kids at risk."

I bit my lip, staring at Dallas in awe.

"I'm sorry for those things. I swear to you if I could go back in time and change things, I would. Not just for you or for me, but for Morgan because she's suffered a lot over the years and I'd give anything to ease that for her."

Mom looked down, her face turning white. "I think—"

"Please let me finish, ma'am," he said, stepping closer to

the table. "I know you think I'm wrong for Morgan. But, I swear, no one will love and care for your daughter like I will. She could have her pick of good men, but she's the *only* right person for me. Every good memory I have is wrapped in her. Every bad decision I made when I was young was to try to get attention because my mom had left and my dad was drunk every day."

"That's right!" Tom stood, his face turning so red that his ears glowed. "You weren't good enough for Morgan then and you're not good enough for her now. You don't belong here in this country club and you're embarrassing this good family."

"That's where you're wrong." Dallas glared at him, pointing a finger. "You're the one who isn't good enough for her. I don't care if you have a high-powered job or gazillions of dollars in the bank. Because when it comes down to it none of that matters. What's important is how you treat the people you love."

"You say that because you have nothing," Tom spat out.

"I have Morgan's best interest at heart. That's more than I can say for you."

Dad's lips compressed as he stood. "You were unfaithful to my daughter while you were dating, Tom? That's your idea of being good enough for her?"

"Not even close." Connor coughed into his hand. "Dallas may have changed enough not to deck you right now, Tom. But I can't say the same about me. It's time for you to take a hike."

"I'm not standing for any more of this," Tom sputtered, looking at each of us incredulously as if he thought we were making a big mistake. But it wasn't until I wiggled my fingers at him and mouthed, "Buh-bye," that he finally stormed off.

I stood up then, moving toward Dallas and stopping in

front of him. "I can't believe you came here tonight after everything I said to you by the Falls."

He lifted my hands. "I love you, Morgan. I always have and I always will. I'm sorry I didn't keep you from falling in the river the other night."

My eyes watered. "But you dove in after me and then pulled me out. That's pretty heroic."

"It wasn't enough." He sucked in a breath, shaking his head. "But I'll do better to keep you safe from here on out. I won't let anything happen to you."

Tears slipped down my face. "I can take care of myself."

"I know," he said, the corner of his mouth lifting. "It took me a while to be good enough to deserve you, but I've always been yours. Always will be."

I smiled through my tears. "I've always been yours, too."

Mom stood up. "Dallas . . ."

He turned to my mom. "I swear I won't hurt her, Mrs. Reed. Give me a chance to prove that to you."

"Call me Ivy." She gave him a nod, then waved to someone behind us. "You'll need a jacket from the hostess if you're going to join us for dinner now. Country club rules."

Dallas paused a moment, seeming choked up, before he finally said, "Yes, ma'am."

"Thanks, Mom," I said, pure joy flowing through me. Dallas squeezed my hands, swinging them back and forth as I stared into his beautiful caramel-colored eyes. Then I wrapped my arms around him and held him tight. "I love you," I whispered. When I finally pulled back, he gave me a smile before he leaned down and pressed a soft kiss to my lips.

We kissed softly and sweetly in front of my family, in front of the wait staff and in front of every single member of the country club. Applause rang out from somewhere and I knew I should pull back because—hello?—my folks were sitting *right* there. But there were no more secrets in this family. I loved this man and I was going to show my true self. Finally.

Dallas was the one who pulled back. "Thank you for letting me crash your dinner."

The hostess, clearly confused by Tom's hasty exit and this rather public display of love, gasped out, "Sir? Would you lift your arms please, so I can slip on your jacket?"

I burst into laughter. His arms were around me and I doubted he wanted to let go. I didn't want to let go, either. I smiled up at him. "Better put that jacket on before every oldster in the place has a heart attack. We'd be killing off half their customer base."

"We can't have that," he said, the corner of his mouth hitching upward. He shrugged into the jacket, looking amazingly hot.

Dad put a hand up, gesturing to someone. "Nina, would you please bring our guest a fresh glass of tea, and a fresh setting?"

Nina's smile was wide and her eyes were wet. For a moment, I wondered if it was because she felt sorrow over Dallas having chosen me but then I realized she was touched by the whole wonderful moment. She hurried off and Dallas sat in Tom's hastily vacated seat.

Dad cleared his throat. "I wish I'd known the truth of why you punched that Tom a long time ago. I might've spared you the trouble and done it myself."

"William!" Mom shook her head, but the glance she gave Dad was fond. "Honey, you're too old for those kinds of things."

He looked at her and his smile was radiant. "I seem to remember that I punched a boy who'd done you wrong back in our day."

My eyes rounded. "You did, Dad? Really?"

Mom fluttered her hands. "Ancient history. Now, what are we thinking for an appetizer?"

With "I'll be Home for Christmas" playing on the speakers and my family surrounding me, I smiled up at the man I loved. His hand found mine under the table and we laced our fingers together. I'd come all the way home, at last.

CHAPTER TWENTY-TWO

On Christmas Eve, my parents' living room oozed festive cheer. The massive Christmas tree stood in the living room, shining with perfectly arranged lights and ornaments. The room was all designer furniture and expensive art on the walls. The presents under the tree had been sorted and stacked to maximize the beauty of the wrappings and ribbons.

I winked at Dallas and withdrew a few strands of tinsel from my pocket and then draped them on the backside of the tree, while I held my breath so my laughter wouldn't give us away.

"If she blames me for that, I'm selling you out," he said, tickling me until I laughed and then pulling me into his arms.

"Fair enough," I said, giggling as I nuzzled his neck, inhaling the deliciously woodsy scent that was all him. Yum.

Connor came into the room with a pitcher of steaming cider. "Tinsel, Morgan? You're aware that Mom's going to blame me, right?"

I shrugged. "She'll never see it."

Mom entered the room, wearing a red sweater and black

slacks, and carrying a tray of sugar cookies that gave off a heavenly scent. "I won't see what?"

"Nothing!" Connor, Dallas, and I said at the same time.

"Oh, you kids. I'll find out sooner or later, you know." Mom set the cookies on the side table next to a silver-framed picture of Grace. She smiled fondly at the photo and then straightened a few throw pillows on the leather couch.

"Do I hear laughter going on in here?" Dad said, coming into the room. He had forsaken his usual suit and tie for a green sweater with a brown reindeer in the center, a red nose, and gold bells dangling off its antlers. "What am I missing?"

Mom's lips twisted. "You can't be serious, William. Where on earth did you get that sweater?"

"Secret Santa at work." Dad tugged at the hem. "Don't you love it? Perfectly festive for Christmas Eve, right?"

I broke into laughter. "Dad, that sweater's awful."

He sighed. "I had a feeling you wouldn't appreciate it."

Connor groaned. "I'll have to find out who your Secret Santa was and get them back next year by giving them a reindeer sweater gift of their own."

"That sounds like just the thing to do, Connor." Mom nodded as if that kind of payback was perfectly acceptable. She took the pitcher of cider from him and arranged it next to the cups already on the coffee table. "Who would like a cup of cider?"

Connor raised his hand. "I'd love one, Mom."

"I'd love one, Ivy," Dallas said.

She gave him a warm smile. "Anyone else?"

Dad and I chimed in that we'd love a cup.

Dallas sat next to me on the couch, lacing his fingers through mine. My folks had invited him for our traditional Christmas Eve gift opening and his being here meant everything to me. It meant they had accepted him, finally, and my heart felt so light and free that I was surprised it didn't float out of my chest and hit the ceiling.

Mom tapped Connor's arm. "Sweetheart, would you poke at the fire, please? I love watching the flames while we open gifts."

Connor dutifully headed to the fireplace while Mom poured five cups of cider. We arranged ourselves on the couch near the tree. I took a cookie and munched on it, letting the sweet and crumbly thing break between my teeth. Delish.

The doorbell rang then and a slight crease appeared between Mom's eyebrows. "It's Christmas Eve. Who could that be?"

I stood. "I'll get it."

I headed for the door and peeked out the peephole. "It's Coraline."

Dallas came up beside me. "Our landlady?"

"Yes." I opened the door and gaped at the woman standing there. Coraline had wild, curly hair that not even the tan bowler hat she'd jammed down on her head could tame. I stared at her, trying not to laugh as I took in her outfit, which included the bowler hat, a pair of beige riding pants, high boots, and a heavy coat over a blue silk blouse accented by colorful scarves.

"Hello, Morgan," she trilled out, pulling me into a hug. "Oh! And, Dallas Parker, you're here on Christmas Eve. How interesting..."

The teasing tone of her voice made me pause as I stepped back. "Um, please come in, Coraline," I said, curious about the smug look on her face.

Coraline stepped into the foyer, trailing scarves behind her. "Hello, Ivy. Love your manicure. Are those snowmen I see?"

"Yes," Mom said, putting a hand to her chest. "Morgan did

them. They're a little more festive than my usual mani, but I thought it would be fun. She's doing my hair next month."

"How wonderful." Coraline waved a tanned hand. "I hear I missed a lot of excitement here in town while I was off on safari. Not that I mind. You have no idea how glorious Africa was, the trip of a lifetime, I tell you. The lions tried to eat us one night, and they did eat one of the tents—and how that played out on their digestive systems is a mystery I don't want to solve. Then there was that pesky rhino that thought our jeep was its toy, but. . . I've gotten off track as to why I'm here tonight. I received a lot of messages from Morgan and Dallas. I seem to have made a *faux pas* and rented my business space to you both."

"Yes," Dallas said, throwing me a questioning look.

I bit my lip. Did he want the business space all to himself? He was so manly that possibly the scent of shampoo and other products all day long was not his thing. But I loved the smell of wood that drifted into my side of the shop. I'd miss it so much if he were gone.

I gulped. "Yes, it was a mistake."

The word tasted bitter and wrong against my tongue.

"Well, that's unfortunate." Coraline tugged her hat so hard it was a wonder her hair didn't blow out the top. "So, does one of you want to break your lease?"

I turned to Dallas, biting my lip. I didn't want to break my lease and I didn't want him to break his either. Once upon a time, I would've done anything to get him out of my rented space and now I couldn't imagine my business without him next door. He shuffled his feet, making me more nervous than ever about that question. What if he wanted to go?

His forehead creased. "I'm not sure how Morgan feels, but it would be difficult to uproot my store at this point. That furniture is heavy and I don't know if any other space would be quite as perfect. And her part of the space seems to be pretty perfect, as well."

I nodded enthusiastically. "I agree. Our businesses are good the way they are. I don't know how you made such a mistake, Coraline, but I called you to ask and . . ." A strange thought halted me and I blinked. "Come to think of it, how *did* you manage to make such a big mistake? I just remembered that I looked at his lease that first day and it was dated well before mine."

Coraline tried for innocence. "Was it? Silly me."

I advanced on her. "Yes, and not by a day or two either. Almost two full weeks earlier than mine."

Coraline burst into laughter. Her eyes danced. "Well, maybe my good friend Melody King told me Morgan was coming back to town and she might've mentioned what a cute couple you two would make, but that you both were stubborn and might need a push."

"Ms. King told you that?" I asked, glancing at Dallas whose mouth had curved upward. I should've known. I'd have to remember to thank my loving mentor on Christmas night when all of us girls sang for her at the extravaganza.

"Merry Christmas to you all!" Coraline tossed a scarf over her shoulder. "I must be going now that the lease situation is settled. I have so much unpacking to do. You wouldn't believe the amount of things one can accumulate on an African safari."

Dallas and I walked Coraline out to her car and she left in a flutter of scarves and words about how great the businesses we'd opened together were doing. We stood in the driveway looking at each other. His eyes crinkled at the corners. "Well, then."

I burst into more laughter. "I don't even know what to say."

He opened his mouth to answer, but then shut it and

leaned toward me. He touched my hair, turning a few strands over with his fingers. Then he looked up at the sky. "Looks like you're getting that miracle."

I blinked. "Say what?"

"Snow," he said, and then drew me into his arms.

"Really?" I looked up and saw tiny white flakes whirling down from the cloudy sky. "The first snowfall of the year," I said, giggling with delight.

"I'd like to give you a present now, if that's okay," he said, brushing the backs of his fingers along my jawline and making my skin hum. "It's private."

"Oh, really?" I grinned, my belly doing a cartwheel. "You do know that my mom probably got the binoculars out and is staring at us through the windows right now."

"I hope not. If she gets too close to the backside of the tree, she's bound to see the tinsel," he joked, drawing a small package from his pocket and then handing it to me.

"You didn't have to get me anything," I said, hoping he loved the gingerbread kit I had wrapped under the tree for him. I fingered the silver box before opening the lid. Then my throat tightened at what lay inside: a hand-carved wooden angel ornament. She was delicate and beautiful, with a small golden plate beneath her feet inscribed, "Forever Yours." My vision blurred. "She's so beautiful."

"You've always been *my* angel," he whispered, tucking my hair behind my ear, and then dropping his forehead to mine. "I thought you could put that ornament on our tree next year. Maybe one day, we'll even have little angels of our own."

"Oh, Dallas," I said, lifting my lashes and peering into those warm caramel-brown eyes. "There's nothing in the world that I'd love more."

The snow began to fall harder, dusting the world with a sugar-colored frosting. My heart warmed and I let my lips find his. That kiss held everything I wanted to say. That I loved him. That I'd always loved him. And that I hadn't just come home to Christmas Mountain. I'd come home to him and I would never leave again.

The End

If you enjoyed spending time
with these characters,
be sure to read Faith's story in:

'Twas the Kiss Before Christmas
(Christmas Mountain Romance Series, 2)

** To receive a FREE BOOK , sign up for
Susan's Newsletter:
susanhatler.com/newsletter **

ABOUT THE AUTHOR

SUSAN HATLER is a *New York Times* and *USA TODAY* bestselling author, who writes humorous and emotional contemporary romance and young adult novels. Many of Susan's books have been translated into German, Spanish, French, and Italian. A natural optimist, she believes life is amazing, people are fascinating, and imagination is endless. She loves spending time with her characters and hopes you do, too. You can reach Susan here:

Facebook: facebook.com/authorsusanhatler
Instagram: instagram.com/susanhatler
Twitter: twitter.com/susanhatler
Website: susanhatler.com
Blog: susanhatler.com/category/susans-blog

TITLES BY SUSAN HATLER

Do-Over Date Series
Million Dollar Date
The Double Date Disaster
The Date Next Door
Date to the Rescue
Fashionably Date
Once Upon a Date
Destination Date
One Fine Date
The Date Mistake

The Wedding Whisperer Series
The Wedding Charm
The Wedding Catch
My Wedding Date
The Wedding Bet
The Wedding Promise

Blue Moon Bay Series
The Second Chance Inn
The Sisterhood Promise
The Wishing Star
The Friendly Cottage
The Christmas Cabin
The Oopsie Island
The Wedding Boutique
The Holiday Shoppe

Better Date than Never Series
Love at First Date
Truth or Date
My Last Blind Date
Save the Date
A Twist of Date
License to Date
Driven to Date
Up to Date
Déjà Date
Date and Dash

Christmas Mountain Romance Series
The Christmas Compromise
'Twas the Kiss Before Christmas
A Sugar Plum Christmas
Fake Husband for Christmas

Treasured Dreams Series
An Unexpected Date
An Unexpected Kiss
An Unexpected Love
An Unexpected Proposal
An Unexpected Wedding
An Unexpected Joy
An Unexpected Baby

Young Adult Novels
See Me
The Crush Dilemma
Shaken

Printed in Great Britain
by Amazon